I0621123

Domination

EXPLICITLY YOURS • BOOK TWO

JESSICA HAWKINS

© 2014 JESSICA HAWKINS
www.JESSICAHAWKINS.net

Editing by Elizabeth London Editing
Proofreading by Tracy Seybold
Cover Design © OkayCreations.
Cover Photo © shutterstock.com/g/kiuikson

Domination (EXPLICITLY YOURS SERIES 2)

All rights reserved. Except as permitted under
the U.S. Copyright Act of 1976, no part of this
publication may be reproduced, distributed, or
transmitted in any form or by any means, or
stored in a database or retrieval system without
the prior written permission of the author.

This book is a work of fiction. Names, characters,
places, and incidents either are products of the
author's imagination or are used fictitiously. Any
resemblance to actual persons, living or dead,
events, or locales is entirely coincidental.

ISBN: 0997869127
ISBN-13: 978-0-9978691-2-5

TITLES BY
JESSICA HAWKINS

LEARN MORE AT JESSICAHAWKINS.NET/BOOKS

SLIP OF THE TONGUE
THE FIRST TASTE
YOURS TO BARE

THE CITYSCAPE SERIES

COME UNDONE

COME ALIVE

COME TOGETHER

EXPLICITLY YOURS SERIES

POSSESSION

DOMINATION

PROVOCATION

OBSESSION

STRICTLY OFF LIMITS

Chapter One

Lola had not had time to think ahead to this moment. She'd never been much of a planner—a fact she'd even prided herself on. Lately she'd been wondering if she'd been wrong, though. She could've set aside some money to start a class or two at the local community college. Or tried harder to find a better job than waitressing at Hey Joe. Maybe then she wouldn't be standing here, about to face her boyfriend of nine years after sleeping with another man for money. All so they'd have a shot at a decent future.

Not just another man. A man who'd seen her on a sidewalk and specifically picked her. He was drawn to her, he'd said—she was a prize, waiting to be claimed by him. At the time, she hadn't known what he'd meant by that. Now she did. It hadn't taken long for her to give in to her attraction to him, but it had to go away now. As if it were a mask she'd slipped on for one night. Or was it that she was putting one back on?

She'd been seduced. She'd been claimed. And then she'd been returned to her doorstep. He wasn't just another man—that was Beau Olivier.

Behind the eggshell-colored door with a brass number six nailed to it, Johnny waited. Johnny and her new life with him. Lola sucked in cool, early-morning air and flushed hot, tainted breath out with her exhale. Apartment six was on the ground floor, just through the gate and within steps of a mold-rimmed pool. All she had to do was turn the key and go home. That, and forget Beau.

The normally finicky lock gave her little resistance. It was dark in the apartment. Thick. Suffocating. Had it always been that way? She opened the shades. Johnny lay lengthwise on the couch, clutching a pillow to his chest. She went and stood over him.

She hadn't thought of Johnny as much as she should've while she was with Beau, but when she had, she'd envisioned him anxiously waiting for her, driving himself slightly insane. Apparently she'd been wrong. If she'd been any later than sunrise, which was when Beau had promised to return her, Johnny might not've even known. She didn't think it was much to ask that after what she'd done for him, Johnny make sure she arrived home safely and on time.

She dropped her purse near his head, and he woke with a start. "Shit—Lola?" He blinked up at her rapidly as if she were an apparition. "Is it over?"

She offered her palms. "I'm here, aren't I?"

He rubbed his eyes and got up on an elbow, tossing the pillow aside. "I'm—I must've fallen asleep. Sorry."

She picked up an empty bottle of Jack Daniels from the floor. "You drank the rest of this by yourself?"

"When I got home from Mark's."

"Mark's?" she repeated, unsure she'd understood him. There'd been no discussion of him doing anything other than coming straight home from work. She hadn't even thought it was necessary. "You went out last night?"

"As opposed to sitting here and thinking about what you were doing? Yeah. I didn't want to be alone."

"When did you get home?" Lola shook her head. She didn't have the energy to argue at the moment. "Never mind. I don't even care."

"Are you mad?" he asked. "What was I supposed to do? I'm sorry if—wait, how am I the one apologizing?"

"Why would either of us apologize?" Her tone dropped to a warning level. "Surely you don't expect me to."

Johnny shut his eyes, leaned back against the couch and ran both hands over his face. "No," he said, sighing. "That's not what I meant. I'm still buzzed. Just give me a minute to wake up."

"Take a few. I'll be in the shower."

He peeked at her through his fingers. "You haven't showered?"

Beau had been so adamant about getting her back by sunrise, it was almost as if he hadn't wanted her to shower. And now she had to stand in front of Johnny, thoroughly worked over by Beau. Even from a distance,

3

Beau exercised his control over them. Her throat was suddenly thick. "There wasn't time."

She had to walk away. It would hurt Johnny to see her get upset since she so rarely did. They both had enough to deal with as it was. "If you want to talk, get coffee ready. Otherwise I won't be able to keep my eyes open."

She went directly for the bathroom and turned the shower on hot. The night had been a flash of lightning. Intense, blinding, crackling—and over before she could even blink. One moment the life-changing decision to sleep with Beau weighed heavily on their shoulders. Now, it was done. Had it changed her life? How could it not have?

She and Johnny knew each other better than anyone. Years ago, he'd taken a chance on her. Burly, gruff, but kind-hearted Johnny. He didn't have to put up with the lost girl Lola used to be, because women liked him. He could've had his pick. Lola partied too hard and had little regard for anyone—even herself. Even Johnny. But he'd believed she could be better. Johnny didn't deserve for Lola to be standing in the shower, her mind drifting away from him.

Drifting to Beau, to his hands, cock and mouth between her legs. His forbidden words in her ear. He liked her tight. He liked her helpless on her hands and knees. He liked her with a red ass. And he was everywhere on her.

She shouldn't have been thinking of any of that. Johnny was in the next room. She was being torn in different directions. The last twelve hours came down on her at once. Big, hot tears mingled with the stream of water. She'd betrayed Johnny with more than just her body—in ways she would've never expected possible in just a night. And despite herself, she missed Beau already.

He wanted a second night, but that was greedy. He'd taken too much already and without apology. How much more could she open herself up to?

The bathroom door creaked. She turned to face the wall, wiping her cheeks. "I won't be long."

There was no response. After a shuffle, Johnny turned her by her shoulders and hugged her to his naked chest. It was all she needed for the tears to flow.

"Did he hurt you?" he asked.

"No. I'm just tired."

"Promise me."

She looked up at his tone. In his face was a shadow of how worried he'd been. "He didn't," she said. "Promise."

He ran a hand up and down her back. "I'm sorry, babe. It was a lot to ask of you."

She returned her cheek to his chest and nodded. "It's done, though. Over." She almost told him it was okay to feel angry. Selfishly, that would make it easier for her to be angry. But she felt very much like a house of cards that couldn't take any more weight without collapsing. Later would be a better time for them to get angry.

"Thank you," she said.

"For what?"

"Not being afraid to touch me."

"How could I be? You're my girl." He kissed the top of her head. "I love you."

She almost rose up to kiss him but was afraid he'd pull away. "Please go make coffee," she said, separating from him.

He left the shower. She didn't cry again. She soaped her breasts, behind her ears, under her feet. All the parts Beau had touched. Everywhere. She was owned, just like he'd promised. She rubbed between her legs a little longer than necessary—one second comforting that unfulfilled ache, the next trying to make it stop. Only an hour earlier, Beau had been inside her. She couldn't come, not so in between Beau and Johnny. Her mind and body had been there with Beau, but her heart knew Johnny was minutes away. She wished she'd just been able to fucking come, because now Beau's ache might never go away. She turned off the water.

Johnny returned to wrap her in a towel. He dried her off and patted her hair. "There's coffee in the living room."

She kept the towel around her, and they went to the couch. Johnny sat at one end while she curled her knees to her chest at the other. He was patient while she sipped from the mug.

"I think maybe it's best I don't go into details," she said.

"That bad?" he asked.

"It's just, I've heard some couples do that. After affairs or whatever. Seems stupid to me. Like asking for trouble."

He nodded, looking into his coffee, thinking. "All right. Last thing I want is to make things harder on either of us." He looked up. "But you were safe? Were you scared?"

"In the beginning a little. He took me to Rodeo Drive—"

"Seriously?"

"Only because I couldn't go in jeans. To the fundraiser, I mean—the event I texted you about. But being around all those people actually made things better. It didn't feel like such a dirty secret."

He coughed. "About that last text. I'm sorry. It was selfish of me. I'd already had a drink—"

She glanced up from her coffee. "Text?"

"You didn't read my response?"

She shook her head. "He took my phone away."

"What do you mean he took it away?"

"He had a very particular way of doing things. He didn't like me mentioning your name. When he found out I'd texted you, he took my phone."

"So basically he's a complete dick."

She looked at her handbag. Johnny's last request the night before had been that she not kiss Beau. Had the text been about that? Or had it been something even bigger—maybe an apology that they'd decided to go through with this at all?

"What'd it say?" she asked.

"Nothing. Just continue. Where'd you go after the event?"

His face was red, as if he were embarrassed by the text. She hesitated, but decided not to pursue it. She would read it later. "After? We went for a nightcap. There's this insane, secret speakeasy on Sunset—"

"Heard of it," he said. "Don't know anyone who's been, though."

"It wasn't anything," she said, shrugging too hard in an attempt to seem convincing.

"Right. After that?"

"I think we should stop there."

"Oh." He bobbed his head slowly. "All right. If that's what you want."

Lola did want to tell him, because only he would understand why their next stop had been so strange. That Beau had taken her to a strip club at all was unusual—but that it'd been the same one she'd worked at? If she mentioned it, Johnny would ask why they went there. He'd want to know if she'd danced for him. Cat Shoppe was a sore topic for Johnny, who'd risked their relationship to get her out of there.

"It's what I want," she said, returning her time with Beau into the vault where it belonged.

He looked around the room. She drank more coffee.

"I checked while you were in the shower. The other half of the money still isn't deposited."

"It's the weekend," she said.

"Right, but it would still show as pending. What if he doesn't pay?"

"He will. I trust—"

Johnny looked at the floor. He didn't blink for so long, she thought she should explain. Not that she trusted Beau himself, but that she trusted him to pay. She hadn't meant anything by it.

He put his hand around her ankle and smiled a little. "I'm glad you're home."

"So am I," she said. "But I'm exhausted. I didn't get much…I just think I should lie down."

"I get it," he said, releasing her foot.

She crawled over the couch and kissed his cheek. "Good morning," she said.

"Good night," he said back.

◆ ◆ ◆

Lola had shut the bedroom windows. The California sun could be too much at times. Regardless, when she opened her eyes, daylight sliced straight lines through the shutters.

Beau would be—what? Working? Sleeping her off? She had no idea, because she didn't know him. That was something she'd have to learn to live with, just like the ache between her legs he'd given her. It throbbed for attention, but she refused to take care of it. She couldn't do it without thinking of Beau, and thinking of Beau now when the entire experience was supposed to be over was unfair to Johnny. The idea of Johnny doing it for her made her stomach cramp.

She reached over the side of the bed and took her phone from her purse. Beau had turned it off. She waited for it to start up, then read the text message Johnny had written barely an hour after she'd left the apartment.

This doesn't feel right. Ask him what happens if we change our minds.

A lump formed in her throat. She put the phone back, took it out again and erased the message. She never wanted to read it again.

She stood from the bed and called out for Johnny, surprised he hadn't woken her since they should've left for work already. There was a note on the kitchen table that he'd given her the night off. Underneath, next to a large, scribbled dollar sign was *We're millionaires.*

It was something to celebrate, but she was in too strange of a mood, stuck somewhere between elation and devastation, asleep and awake, Beau and Johnny. It was her first moment completely alone since before Beau had picked her up.

They had their money. Their dream future would soon be a reality. It'd been fun to consider her options, like doing something other than Hey Joe, but now it was final. Why else would she have sold herself if not because she wanted this too? It was hard to stomach the idea that she'd done it all for Johnny like Beau had suggested. *Sacrifice* was the word he'd used—she couldn't *sacrifice* herself for someone else's happiness.

Lola found leftovers in the fridge, ate them with her beer and went back to bed. If Beau was right, she'd been sacrificing herself for a long time. Some part of her had always felt she'd owed Johnny that for taking a chance on her years ago. Now she wondered if that debt would ever feel paid.

Chapter Two

Lola and Johnny's one-bedroom apartment didn't have much space, so the kitchen became their office. Because Johnny had given Lola the night off work to sleep, she woke up earlier than normal on Sunday. She ran out for donuts, made fresh coffee and got to work.

On their dining table, Lola's laptop screen was crowded with information about buying an existing business. When Johnny walked in, she looked up from the notepad she'd been taking notes on.

"Morning," he said, tossing a football in his hand. "You were up early."

She glanced at the football. "What's that for?"

"Game today."

Lola set down her pen. "We're not going to the picnic. We have too much to do."

"I thought we were doing all this tomorrow."

"We are. Today and tomorrow." She gestured at the donuts. "Look, I got all your favorites. They even have the custard filling I never let you get. I'm not above bribery."

He picked one up and bit into it. Multi-colored sprinkles fell onto the table. "But we don't have the details yet," he said, chewing. "We won't until we sit down with Mitch."

"I know, but I want to be prepared *before* we sit down with Mitch. I think we should go in with a plan. Did you know it can take months to transfer a liquor license? We should get started on that now."

"Now—as in right now? Can't it wait until after the game?"

"Six hundred thousand is a little high for a bar on Sunset Boulevard," she continued, ignoring him, "especially one that's struggling like we are. But that's the number Mitch gave me. I think he's factoring in the worth of the brand. We'll have a lot of expenses off the bat too, including the food and liquor licenses. I figure that leaves us with around three hundred grand."

"That's a good cushion," he said, leaning his hands on the back of a chair.

She shook her head. "It's not a cushion, Johnny. If we're doing this, we have to do it right—like renovations to the kitchen that's been out of use for decades. You said you wanted to serve food, so we'll have to go through a health inspection."

Johnny brushed off his hands on his pants. "Sounds like you got this covered."

"I don't," she said. "You know more about running a bar because you love it. I'd rather focus on advertising and marketing, and I'd like a decent budget for that since we're trying to generate new foot traffic."

Johnny set the football on the table. "All right. I see where you're coming from. But I won't be any good to you now. My head's already in the game. So I'll tell you what—why don't we go down to the park, play some football, eat some lunch and chill a little bit. Then tonight I'll tell Mitch neither of us are coming in. That gives us tonight and all day tomorrow."

"We can't just take the night off like that."

"Why not? Not like we're desperate for the money anymore."

"Johnny, you're not hearing me. We need every last cent. I don't want to nag you, but you've got to take this seriously. Running a business is not about doing what you want. It's about buckling down and doing whatever it takes, even on the weekends. It's late hours and waking up earlier." She looked over at the clock. "You can't be sleeping until eleven anymore."

He held up his palms. "I understand this is serious, I promise, but we haven't even sat down with Mitch yet. Let's take a little time to get adjusted."

He ate another donut. She'd already lost him for the morning. Johnny wouldn't be any good to her if she forced him to stay home—as if this had been *her* dream. As if she'd always wanted a bar of her own. She'd have to feed off Johnny's passion to make this work, but he wasn't showing her any.

"Go ahead to the game," she said. "I'm staying here. You really think Mitch'll give us both the night off?"

"It's a Sunday," he said. "They can handle things without us. But, um…"

The look on his face told Lola she was about to hear something she wouldn't like. If he asked her to make potato salad, when the reason she was skipping the picnic was because there was so much to do, she'd really let him have it. "What?" she asked, already irritated.

"Well, I've been thinking about this the last few days. Everybody knows we don't have the money to come in and buy Hey Joe, especially in cash. So the money's got to come from somewhere."

"Okay," she prompted.

"So I got this idea. After the game, I'll call in and tell Mitch there was a death in your family. You didn't hear about it until now because you never knew him, but the guy—let's say your great uncle—left you a huge inheritance."

"No way," Lola said, turning back to her notepad. "That's too fucked up."

"I tell Mitch I have to stay home with you, so it gives us the next couple days off to work on the plan, and it also explains the money. They already know you don't got much family, so it wouldn't be weird that you find out about this long-lost cousin."

"Uncle," Lola corrected.

"Whatever. Lo, how else are we going to explain it?"

Normally Lola's answer would've been the truth— that was a pretty good explanation for most things. But not in this case. She looked up at him again.

He shrugged. "What else? The lottery? A death in the family invites no questions, and it kills two birds with one stone."

"We can't do that," she said. "Mitch, Vero, Quartz—they're like family. What about Mark and Brenda? Are you willing to lie to your best friend about this?"

Johnny looked out the tiny window over the kitchen sink a minute. "Well, then I guess we tell them the truth. You slept with a wealthy guy. Makes me look like a chump, but I'm more worried about you."

Lola had been scribbling absentmindedly on her notepad. They wouldn't get away without an explanation. It was the first she'd thought of it, though. She stopped doodling and gripped the pen. "We can't tell them the truth. So I guess we have no other choice."

"All right, that's settled then. Don't worry about them. I'll take care of it." He came over and squeezed her shoulders. "You seem tense."

"I thought the hard part was over," she said. "But we still have a lot of work ahead of us."

"It'll all come together, babe. Don't stress." He massaged her, and she relaxed back in her seat. "Sure you don't want to come? Just for a few hours?"

"No, it's okay. I'll get everything in order, and we can sit down when you get home."

"Cool. They'll be pissed about the potato salad," he teased.

She smiled a little. Potato salad didn't seem like such a big deal anymore, now that she was lying about a death in her family. "Swing by Pavilions on your way. Nobody'll even know the difference."

He kissed the top of her head and lingered there a moment. "Of course they will. You make it the best." He straightened up, ruffled her hair and left the kitchen.

Lola glanced at her computer screen. When she'd researched Beau before their night together, she'd come across a feature a few years back naming him as one of Los Angeles's top investors in startup companies. Lola searched for the article. Each featured investor had been quoted alongside their stats. At the time, she hadn't given Beau's piece much thought. But now it seemed worth revisiting.

"I'm looking at the people just as much as the project. Without those who are willing to work hard and sacrifice, a company won't make it. There's no lack of good ideas or passion out there, but building something with your own two hands takes endurance."

Beau had passion for his work. She hadn't realized it until they'd talked about it at the gala. He'd also toiled, stayed dedicated, overcome defeat. Regardless of how he flaunted his money or that he'd treated her like a commodity, he'd earned all of his dollars, and there was something to be said for that.

Having passion was the easy part. If she and Johnny didn't even have that, how would they make this work?

◆ ◆ ◆

They went to Mitch that Tuesday afternoon. He listened to their offer, his face more saggy than normal while he stared at them across his desk. When Johnny finished, it was a few moments before anyone spoke.

"I'm just a little…" Mitch seemed to struggle for words. "I didn't really expect you to pull this off. Where's this money coming from?"

"I told you Lola's relative passed away," Johnny said. "He also left her some money."

"I thought you said you found out about him this weekend. You came to me last week and asked me to wait for your offer."

"Well, we found out last week," Johnny said. "We just weren't sure if the money would come through, but it will. It didn't really hit Lola until Sunday, which is why she needed me there."

"Right. Sorry to bring it up. Lola, this is what you want to do with your money?"

"Yes. And it's our money," she said. "This is Johnny's dream. I don't want there to be any question about who's in charge."

"What about you?" Mitch asked.

The night before, Johnny had caught Lola on the Santa Monica College website, browsing through the degree programs. "I'm thinking of going back to school," she'd said.

"But Hey Joe will require all of our time and money now," he'd said. "Your words."

It was true—she'd said that. And school would always be there. But they could end up in trouble if they weren't careful, and neither of them had any business experience. She'd agreed and let it go. She'd already missed registration anyway.

"I'm completely on board," Lola said to Mitch. With or without the education, she was dedicated to making this work. "But Johnny's the one sailing this ship."

"Six hundred K," Johnny said. "That's a pretty sweet offer, Mitch."

"It is, but—"

Lola curled her hands in her lap. "But what? You said that would be enough."

"I did say that, yes. When Walken found out I needed more time because I was hearing another proposal, he upped his offer."

"To how much?" Johnny asked. Lola closed her eyes.

"Eight hundred," Mitch said.

The room was quiet. Lola shook her head and looked at Mitch again. "That's ridiculously high."

Mitch shrugged. "I know."

"I researched the value of nearby businesses," Lola said. "Six hundred was too high. Eight hundred is just…"

"Too much," Mitch said.

"Hank can't possibly think he's getting a deal."

Mitch nodded. "I'm agreeing with you. But I'm going to turn down an extra two hundred because the guy's an idiot?"

"We can do eight hundred," Johnny said.

Lola turned to him. "Johnny—"

"Mitch, listen to me," Johnny said, putting his hands on the edge of the desk. "We'll take it for eight hundred. We've got our hearts set on it. But please don't let Walken drive it any higher. Promise me here, now, as my friend of over twelve years—this is everything I've got."

Mitch sighed. "I can't promise—"

"Mitch." Johnny leaned forward. His fingers pressed down until they were white. "Do you really want to see your dad's place ruined for a little more money? Don't get greedy, man. Don't sell out. You know Lola and I will keep your dad's vision alive."

Johnny was at the edge of his seat, practically falling forward onto his knees. The last time she'd seen him so impassioned was when he was asking her nineteen-year-old self to quit her self-destructive lifestyle so they could be together. This big-picture excitement was what she needed from him, but it had to trickle down to the routine parts of running a business too.

"Son of a bitch," Mitch said. "You'd better not let me down."

"So we have a deal?" Johnny asked, standing.

"Just don't mention that last part to Barb, all right?" Mitch said. "She finds out I could've gotten more money and she'll have my neck."

Lola wasn't sure what to feel. It was what they'd wanted, but that money would cut into their already limited budget.

"I have to tell you, though," Mitch continued, "the landlord's wary of the whole thing. His dad dealt with my dad, and our families have done business since opening day. He wants six months' rent upfront plus a security deposit."

"What's that look like?" Lola asked.

"Deposit is thirty grand, and with half a year's rent you're looking at over a hundred K."

Lola and Johnny exchanged glances. That would mean they'd be going forward with less than a hundred thousand to fall back on. It didn't seem like enough.

"It's not a problem," Johnny said.

Lola touched his forearm. "Maybe we should take a minute and think about this."

"We'll still have enough," he said quietly. "It's not as much as we set aside for renovations, but it's enough to get started."

"What about advertising?"

"We'll worry about that later, once we get some profit coming in." Lola was about to explain there might not be any profits if they couldn't get customers in the door, but Johnny cut her off by reaching out to shake Mitch's hand. "Thanks, man. Really, I mean it."

"Can't wait to see what you do with the place. Why don't you two take the night off? Go do something fun."

"You're giving us *another* night?" Lola asked, raising her eyebrows.

"Just one. As a congratulations." He sat back at his desk. "It could be a while before you both get another night off together."

They thanked Mitch and headed out to the parking lot together. Time alone was just what they needed. It was what they deserved after everything they'd been through.

Johnny surprised Lola by picking her up and spinning her around. "Can you fucking believe it?" he said, grinning. "We're doing it. Buying a goddamn bar."

Lola smiled despite the pit in her stomach. "I think I'm still in shock."

"Not me. I've been ready for years."

"We should change the name to Hey Johnny," she joked.

He chuckled, squeezing her. "I wish. Where should we celebrate? And don't say a bar."

She also laughed.

"God, I love your laugh," he said. "Always have."

"Johnny," she said, burying her face in his neck. He could still catch her off guard and make her blush. He was happy, and even though she worried, she was happy too. That eased the pit in her stomach a little.

◆ ◆ ◆

Lola owned one dress for such a special occasion— fitted but not flashy, sheer from her neck to her cleavage, including the sleeves to her elbows. Black, of course. She'd worn it once for Johnny's kid sister's college graduation party.

She came out of the bathroom, all fixed up. Johnny pushed hangers around the closet, still in his underwear.

"Babe?" she asked. Normally he was ready in half the time it took her.

"Don't have anything to wear," he muttered. "I'll have to get some new things."

"What you've got is fine, Johnny. You don't have to dress up."

He looked over his shoulder at her, up and down. "I've never seen that dress before."

"Yes, you have. I wore it to Natasha's graduation."

"Oh." He turned back to the closet. "Well, I'd call that pretty dressed up. I can't exactly show up in jeans when you're wearing that."

"I can change," she said. It made no difference to her. She wasn't even the one who'd chosen the restaurant, an expensive steakhouse in Beverly Hills they'd read about in the paper a few weeks earlier.

"No, don't. You look too pretty." He pulled out a checkered, long-sleeved button down. "How's this? Also what I wore to her graduation."

"It's—" She turned toward the kitchen when her phone rang. "That shirt's great, honey," she called as she left the room. "You look good in red."

She found her cell in her purse, and her heart leapt at the unknown number. It couldn't be him, though. Beau was not allowed to just sneak up on her that way—not when it was so important that she put him behind her. With a quick glance back toward the bedroom, she answered it and held her breath.

"Lola," there was a pause on the line, "are you there, *ma chatte*?"

She placed the phone over her chest, then pulled it away, worried he'd hear her nervous heartbeat. She went out the front door, closed it quietly behind her and put her cell to her ear again. "What do you want?"

"You haven't given me an answer," Beau said.

"I told you no in the car that morning."

"You discussed it with Johnny?"

She hesitated. Before her first night with Beau, she'd been stronger. She was able to see clearer. She hadn't told Johnny about Beau's second offer. If Johnny made her decide again, she had a feeling she knew what her answer would be. It was better not to ask the question at all. "You shouldn't be calling me."

He made a low, humming noise that reminded her of his mouth between her legs. "Don't change the subject."

"It doesn't matter what Johnny says. The answer is no."

"Have you bought the bar yet?"

The change of topic took her a moment to register. "Yes. Well, no. We gave our offer, and now it's just a matter of paperwork."

"Do you have a lawyer?"

"Johnny's cousin is one."

"Johnny's cousin," Beau repeated to himself. "Who will represent you?"

"What? There is no me. There's only me and Johnny."

"You need representation too."

"No, I don't. And even if I did, it's none of your business."

They were quiet a moment. She pictured Beau in his office at the end of the day. He could've been at home, but he sounded tense. Maybe Lola brought that out in him, though. It seemed they were frequently on the verge of arguing.

"I'll have my lawyer contact you," he said finally. "He'd keep only your best interests in mind. My treat."

"I can't go to Johnny with my own lawyer. That's absurd."

"Are you buying the place together?"

"Yes."

"So your name will go on everything?"

"Yes, but it's Johnny's baby."

"How will you share the profits? Fifty-fifty? What if you break up?"

"Break up?"

"That's why you need someone looking out for you."

"I have someone," Lola said softly. "Johnny. We aren't breaking up."

"I just want you to be careful. Smart. You've never had money like this to complicate things."

She'd only had the money a few days, but that was turning out to be true. Before Beau had walked into their lives, things had been simple. Now, every day came with a new problem that was above her and Johnny's heads and new tension between them.

"Money's supposed to make life easier," she said.

"It doesn't. People think that, but they don't realize there are downsides to wealth."

"Are you calling to talk me out of taking the deal?"

"So you're considering it then?"

"No. I didn't mean it like that." Or had she? Was she considering it? A night like the one they'd had could never be duplicated. It also couldn't be forgotten. It was tempting enough to wonder what would even happen during a second night, much less actually consider it.

"I should go," she said.

"Don't sign anything without having someone read it over first."

Lola suppressed a smile. "So that's why you called. To hound me about a lawyer?"

"Yes." He sighed. "No. Not really. Your voice—I missed it. Has anyone ever told you how comforting it can be?"

He'd spoken it softly, as if it were their private secret. They had enough secrets, though. Having breakfast in bed—it felt like a secret. Her willingly opening her legs to him? Secret. They were things that couldn't leave the presidential suite. And this conversation needed to end before it went any further. "Beau—"

"I wish you were here now to whisper to me."

Lola looked over her shoulder again. She remembered him whispering to her, not the other way around. Telling her how it felt to be inside her, how tight and hot and wet she was. Her heart clenched longingly. With Beau, it didn't take much to draw her in.

"What…what would you have me say?" she asked.

"I wouldn't have you say anything. What fun is that? I'd want you to say whatever comes to you."

That ache returned between her legs—or maybe it'd never left. It still hadn't been taken care of. "'Goodbye, Beau.' That's what comes to me."

"I won't stop until I get the answer I want," he warned. "Talk to him."

She shook her head, ended the call and looked around the courtyard. The complex was muted by dusk. Beau's voice was more intense on the phone. Bolder. Huskier. He'd said "whisper to me" suggestively, with promise, as if he knew she would be doing it soon.

"Beau," she whispered aloud to the silence. She felt his weight on her again, his chest to her back, slick with a sheen of their sweat. His mouth at her ear, his hot breath, his even hotter words.

The apartment door opened behind her, and she whirled around so fast she almost lost her footing.

Johnny held his arms wide open. "How do I look?" he asked, showing off his shirt.

Her heart raced as though she'd been caught doing something wrong. "You look," she cringed, but the words were already falling out of her mouth, "like a million bucks."

Chapter Three

Lola stepped out of the car as the door opened for her. She was greeted by the valet's smile. Johnny came around the hood to meet her.

"Sorry about the car," Johnny said to the young man. "It's old. Probably a lot shittier than you're used to."

The valet shrugged. "It's fine. You should see my ride."

Johnny nodded ardently at that. "Yeah. Cool."

Lola waited until they were out of earshot, just before they entered the steakhouse. "Don't apologize for something as stupid as our car," she said. Their car had seen better days, and it was a stick shift, but it didn't merit an apology. "Like the valet really gives a crap about anything other than his tip."

"Oh, I'll give him one hell of a tip. Just don't want anyone thinking we're going to dine and dash or something."

"Nobody thinks that. Do I really look that out of place?"

He rolled his eyes. "You know I didn't mean it like that."

"You make it sound like I shouldn't eat here because I'm not wearing a designer dress."

"All right, all right," he said with exasperation. He took her hand. "You made your point."

Lola was beginning to see how a sudden influx of cash could go to someone's head—except that in her mind, there was no cash. It was almost all promised away. "Sometimes it's good to let people underestimate you," she said.

The hostess greeted them warmly, smiling as she complimented Lola's dress. Lola tried not to look smug as they were led to their table. "We're so honored you've chosen to dine here this evening," the woman said. "We hope it exceeds your expectations. If you need anything at all, please let your server or me know."

"We should hire her," Johnny said when she excused herself. "It's nice to make your guests feel special."

"We can start calling Quartz 'Mr. Quartz.'"

"And we'll replace all the glasses with crystal ware."

"And we'll finally put in a new toilet so it doesn't make that gurgling noise anymore."

"Let's not get carried away," Johnny said, laughing.

The waiter was just as friendly, making small talk as he laid black napkins in their laps.

"We'll take the most expensive champagne you've got," Johnny said without even opening the menu.

"Johnny," Lola said. "That's not necessary."

He glanced from the waiter to her. "We can afford to splurge for once in our lives, Lola."

"But it's champagne. Really. It'll be gone by the end of the night. Let's get a nice, reasonable bottle of red wine."

"Shall I come back?" the man asked.

"No," Johnny said. "Bring the champagne."

Lola looked up at the server. "Can you give us a minute?"

"Certainly."

"No champagne," Lola said firmly while he walked away. "It's excessive."

"Listen to me." Johnny leaned forward on his elbows, twining his fingers. "One *million* dollars. You comprehend that, right?"

She blinked slowly. "Are you seriously asking me that?"

"Okay, but—"

"And it's not a million anymore," Lola continued. "Once this deal goes through and we have to pay that rent, we've got barely anything left."

"It's still a ton of money, Lo. More than we've ever had. I'll talk to the landlord and get us out of paying upfront."

"It's not a ton of money. I told you we needed all the extra help we could get. Aside from the big things, there's maintenance, and wages and all the other expenses that come with owning a business." Lola's breath wasn't coming as fast as she needed. The reality of their commitment came crashing through the dream, right down onto her shoulders. "Honestly, a million's not even enough for what we just agreed to."

"Lola, honey. Calm down. I'm not asking to take a vacation, all I'm saying is for this one night, we can afford to—"

"Do you think I fucked a stranger for a bottle of champagne?"

The tables around them got quiet, but Lola kept her eyes on Johnny as her words hung in the air.

"Christ," he said. "You really believe that's what I think? That might be the shittiest thing you've ever said to me."

She covered her mouth. "Oh, God. You're right."

"You can quit staring," Johnny said to someone behind her. "Nothing to see here."

Lola's phone chimed with a text message. She pulled it out to see the same unknown number that she'd answered earlier.

You're still here with me. Say yes.

"Who is it?" Johnny asked.

"No one." She put the cell away. "Brenda about this weekend." Lola stood. "I just need a minute alone."

"No. Sit."

She looked at the table and sat back in her chair.

"The last few days, you've left the room in the middle of our conversations more times than I can count. What's going on?"

Sometimes it was all just too much to take in. Johnny was so happy about the bar. She was happy for him. She couldn't seem to get further than that.

While they'd been seated at the kitchen table Sunday night, working on their plan, she'd glanced up once to find Johnny staring at her. She knew what was on his mind, but she was too afraid to bring it up. What did he think happened that night? Was the truth better or worse than his imagination?

"Hey," Johnny said, calling her back from the memory. "Forget about the champagne. What're you thinking right now?"

"I feel guilty," she said quietly. "You're hurting. And it's my fault."

"No. We went into this together." He craned his neck to catch her eye. "Didn't we, Lo? Start to finish, you and me. Have I given you any reason to think I'm hurt?"

"You've been so supportive." He had been, in his own way. He didn't judge her or put the blame on her. He was quiet, but that didn't mean he wasn't there for whatever she needed. "Somewhere inside, though, you must be angry."

He sighed, working his jaw back and forth. "I try not to think about it. I think about the money and us. As long as I focus on you and me and what's ahead of us, I'm okay."

She tried not to think of it either, but Beau's grip on her—his large, enveloping hands physically on her body but also the unwavering way he demanded her attention—would flash over her without warning.

Sometimes that was the real reason she had to leave the room. Johnny had been so calm about it all, but his lack of reaction was beginning to worry her. "If you thought about it," she said, "how would it make you feel?"

"Crazy. Hurt." He looked away for one quick second. "And yes, angry. But none of that is directed at you."

"Are you sure?"

"Yeah. Those feelings will go away, I just need a little time."

"If you had a second chance at the money, would you take it?"

"You mean would I have said yes, knowing what I know now?" He spun his water glass on the table. "I can't really answer that, babe. I don't know what you went through. I mean, look at what we did today. I never thought handing over that much money would be one of the best moments of my life, but there it is. Even though we didn't yet—I already feel like I finally own something. And that something will mean a better life for my girl."

She pressed her palms together in her lap. "That's not what I was asking."

"What then?"

The damp spot on the tablecloth grew while Johnny absentmindedly played with his water glass. She'd decided not to bring it up for a reason. The plan was that she'd never see Beau again, but his voice was still in her ear. He expected her to say yes. To submit to him another night. "Never mind," she said. "I shouldn't have said anything."

"Said anything about what? Look at me."

She met his puzzled eyes. "He made me another offer, Johnny."

"Who?"

"You know who." She chewed her bottom lip. "I told him no."

"He made you another *offer*?" He rubbed his forehead, shaking his head. "I don't understand. When?"

"The morning after, when I was getting out of the car."

He dropped both forearms on the table and fixed his attention on her. "That was days ago. Why am I only hearing about this now?"

"I didn't want to make things worse."

"Worse?" he asked, raising his voice. "That's not fair. Have I been anything other than completely understanding through all of this?"

"You've been amazing," she said, her head lowered.

"If anyone has secrets, it should be you and me. Not you and him."

"It wasn't a secret, I just—"

"Don't. Stop."

She lifted her eyes again.

He leaned in. "I don't think you *understand* how *understanding* I've been. I didn't go crazy. I haven't treated you differently since then." He pointed to his chest. "I don't deserve to be shut out."

"You haven't said no yet," Lola pointed out.

He sat back against his chair and crossed his arms. "I mean, what the fuck am I supposed to say to that? What exactly went on that he'd pay another million for you?"

"Johnny," she exclaimed. His words sent a stabbing pain through her stomach. Apparently, he was just as capable as Beau of making her feel cheap.

"No," he said. "I want to know. If this is on the table, I need to know what happened that night. What exactly he got for his money. Where he took you."

Her mouth fell open. "We agreed—"

"I did that for you. You don't think I want to know the truth? It drives me insane wondering what a million dollars bought that prick."

"Stop." Lola's throat was so thick, she couldn't catch a breath. "I feel sick."

"Yeah?" He banged his fist on the table. "Well, so do I."

"Sir," the waiter said, hurrying over. "I have to ask you—"

"I knew it," Johnny said. He threw his napkin on the table and stood. "I'm sorry we're not good enough for your fifty-dollar steak. We'll go."

"I didn't say that, sir. Absolutely not—we value your business. I was just going to ask you to keep it down."

"Johnny, just sit," Lola pleaded.

"I have to get out of here." He walked away.

"I'm so sorry," Lola said to the waiter, grasping for her purse from the floor. "I can pay."

"For what?" he asked. "Bread and water?"

"I don't know. I'm just so sorry."

"Don't be." He smiled. "You aren't the first couple to fight before appetizers."

She thanked him. His graciousness reinforced her idea that people from all walks of life had money, and she and Johnny had as much right to be there as anyone. It was an effort, but she kept her eyes up as she made her way through the tables to the exit.

The valet stood from his station when he saw her.

"Did my boyfriend just come out here?" she asked.

"Guy with the ponytail? He just left."

"With the car?"

"Yes, ma'am."

Lola looked down at her dress and heels. Johnny wasn't the type to abandon her, which meant he just hadn't thought of her at all. She wasn't sure which was worse. No matter how you looked at it, she had no way of getting home, and she wasn't even wearing clothes she felt comfortable in. That was Johnny's fault.

"Asshole," she muttered. She took out her phone to call him. Beau's text was still on the screen.

You're still here with me. Say yes.

She read it again. *Here with me.* Their night had gone so fast, it was almost as if it hadn't happened at all. Except that once in a while, she *was* still there with Beau, reliving their moments together. She'd seen Mayor Churchill on TV that morning and remembered holding Beau's hand in the crowd at the benefit. On the way to the restaurant earlier, Nirvana had been on the radio, and Lola had hummed along, back at the speakeasy.

She moved her finger to hover over his phone number. It wasn't long ago they'd talked. With a tap, she could call Beau to come get her. Maybe he still had the hotel room. It shouldn't have even been an option, but it was—and a luxurious one at that. She knew with certainty that Beau would come, just like she knew he wouldn't have left her behind in the first place.

She cleared the text and called Johnny instead.

◆ ◆ ◆

It was after two in the morning when Lola heard noises outside their apartment. She stood from the couch. "I've been trying to get ahold of you," she said before the door was even open. "Where have you been?"

Johnny toed off his shoes and left them by the door. "Thinking."

"Drinking?" she asked.

"No. Just thinking."

"I was worried."

"I know," he said. "I was also worried. About you."

"Serves you right for leaving me there," she said.

"I had to get away before I said something I regretted."

She fell back onto the couch. "I know." She'd been angry for the first few hours. The whole cab ride home, she'd been tempted to give the driver the address to Beau's hotel. If he'd been there, Beau would've made sure she was comfortable, and that sounded appealing after the week she'd had. But her anger had turned to concern around midnight. Now she was just glad Johnny was home safely.

He came to her and bent to take her cheeks in his hands. He kissed her. "You're always so good. So understanding. What did I do to deserve you?"

"Sit, Johnny. We should talk."

He sat close to her and held her hand. "I know what we agreed on, but if I'm going to consider this, I need to know what happened that night. I can't send you back in there if I don't."

So he *would* send her in to do their dirty work again. Lola rested her elbow on the arm of the couch as she leaned away a little. Even if she'd been fighting the desire to see Beau again, she was disappointed Johnny was fine enough with the first night that he'd let her do a second. She'd worried telling him might make him think she wanted to do it, but apparently he just wanted details. If she were a spiteful person, she'd give them to him. Johnny wasn't built for details.

"What makes you think I'd do it again?" she asked.

"You brought it up. I figured if you weren't considering it…you would've kept it to yourself."

"I brought it up because I thought you should know."

"Yes, right after you brought up money. I hate to admit it, but maybe we are in over our heads."

"We can still call the whole thing off," she said. "We don't have to buy Hey Joe. We could do something else."

"I can't." He shook his head. "You didn't endure what you did so I could give up before we even got started."

She swallowed at the word *endure*. It wasn't the word she would've chosen, which was why a second night of it could be dangerous. "I don't want you to give up. We'll just have to get creative and take on as many tasks as we can so we don't have to pay other people."

He released her hand and put his arm along the back of the sofa. "Can't believe I'm saying this, but a million dollars is a hell of a lot less money than I thought."

"But it's not nothing," she said. "Maybe we could even take out a loan in the beginning."

"True."

She waited. "That's it? 'True'?"

He pulled on the corner of a cushion but didn't look away from her. "You keep saying how we need every last dollar. How it's not enough. And you—you already did it once. We can never take that back. Once the line is crossed, it's crossed."

She watched him closely. To her, a second night was not the same as a first night. It meant sinking deeper into Beau and the way she felt when she was with him, but there was no way of explaining that to Johnny. "What are you saying?"

"I guess that if you look at it from a strictly business point of view—this kind of money for a few hours is unheard of. You'd already know what you were in for. We sort of already broke the seal off this deal."

"Looking at it from a strictly business point of view makes me feel like a prostitute," she said flatly. He still hadn't said no. She couldn't tell if that was a yes. "Is that how you see me?"

A red splotch appeared on Johnny's neck. "A *prostitute?* God, no." He got off the couch and kneeled in front of her. He took her stiff, tense hands in his warm ones. "If that's how you feel, of course we won't do it. What we have now will be enough." He kissed the backs of her hands. "How did we even get in this mess?"

"I have no idea," she said.

Johnny looked at her earnestly. She put a hand on his face.

"Feel better?" he asked, smiling up at her.

She averted her eyes—she didn't feel better. Beau's offer had only been on the table a few hours, but she'd already begun to think about how it would be to see him again. Yes, she had an idea of what a second night would have in store, but Beau also had ways of surprising her. The possibilities were endless.

No, the possibilities *would've* been endless.

Johnny stood up. They held each other's gaze a minute. "So it's decided," he said, turning.

"Wait, Johnny." She grabbed his hand.

He looked back at her.

She put her lips to his knuckles. "Johnny," she whispered. Her hand fit perfectly in his. *Remember this?* A gentle touch to love her. Fingers that had been everywhere on her body, over and over.

His eyes traveled from her face to their hands. "You think this is a good idea?"

"I don't know." She pulled him back down to the couch and let go of him to lift her tank top over her head. It left her bare from the waist up. He looked. She leaned over to undo his slacks before climbing onto his lap.

"You…" He kept his eyes on her breasts.

"What, Johnny?" she asked. What did he need? Reassurance of her love? To know if he'd been a better lover than Beau? She grew hungrier by the second. She'd had sex on her mind since she'd left Beau, but she hadn't wanted to make the first move. "Ask me anything, and I'll answer."

He cleared his throat. "He showed you his test results, right?"

Lola stilled. It wasn't what she'd expected. It was something a man should never have to ask his girlfriend, even if it was a perfectly reasonable—almost necessary—question for their situation. "Yes. He's clean."

"Okay." He looked up finally. "What?"

"Nothing." Right before they made love was not the time to anguish over the heartbreak of a question like that. She forgot it and set her palms against his shirt. "Put your arms around me."

He did, pulling her closer by her backside.

"Stop thinking," she said.

He kissed her. She settled her hips to get closer to him as she unbuttoned his shirt. She reached between them, felt for him, rubbed him. And rubbed him harder, until he also reached down to move her hand away.

"I think I need more time," he said. "My mind keeps going somewhere it shouldn't."

"I'm still me, Johnny."

"I know." He kissed her, and he was present. His forehead rested against hers. "I know. Can you just say it out loud? Maybe it will help."

"Say what out loud?"

"That you did it. You never even said you did it."

"How would that help?"

"I don't know. Can you…?"

Her eyes fell to the exposed skin at the base of his neck. She hadn't said it. Maybe it'd been intentional, because she was having trouble getting the words out. "I slept with him. That was the deal."

His chest rose and fell. He nodded. "I know. I don't know why I wanted to hear it."

"It's all right." She dipped her head to get him to look at her. "We're in uncharted waters here. You can always tell me what you need."

"So good," he whispered. "So understanding."

"I'm trying," she whispered back. "I know you are too." The resignation in his eyes was too much to handle. She'd forgotten that for her, all of this was real from the moment she'd gotten into that limo—but Johnny had never had that moment. He was in limbo somewhere between making the deal and getting her back. "You must be hungry," she said, the only fix she could offer at that moment.

"Not really."

"I can make you a sandwich."

He shook his head. "It's okay. I'm sorry I ruined dinner."

"I heard fifty-dollar steak sucks anyway." They both laughed a little. "However, I happen to make a mean peanut butter and jelly sandwich." She winked. "And all it'll cost you is one kiss."

Chapter Four

Vero poured two shots and slid one down the bar. Lola caught it and drank it down in a gulp. "What was that for?" she asked, sending back an empty glass.

"Think you need it. Should I get Johnny one?"

"Why?"

"Think he needs it too."

Lola turned to lean her hip against the bar. "What do you mean?"

"He's been staring at you the way I see the regulars stare at a new woman in this bar. Like he wants to meet you but doesn't know what to say."

"Need a pitcher of Fat Tire," Amanda called over the bar.

"Got it." Vero got started on the order as Amanda walked away. "You and Johnny all right?"

"We're fine," Lola said. Since their steak dinner the night before was a bust, they'd splurged on gourmet hamburgers for lunch that day. It was a fraction of the cost of the steak, but it was them, and that was the most important thing. They'd had a little too much beer and sun followed by a nap. Beau and his offer hadn't come up. She'd thought it was nearly the perfect afternoon, but when she woke up, Johnny had left for work without her.

"You roleplaying something kinky?" Vero pressed on. "Like the whole stranger in a bar thing? If so, I'm cool with it. Maybe I can help."

Lola laughed, shaking her head. "Well, we're not really supposed to talk about it, but you're impossible to shut up."

Vero set the pitcher on the bar and turned to face Lola. "This sounds real kinky. Lay it on me."

"No, it's not that." Lola lowered her voice. "Johnny and I are buying Hey Joe." Lola grinned at Vero's expression. She wasn't sure she'd ever seen Vero's mouth open with nothing coming out.

"Are you messing with me?" Veronica asked.

"Nope. We're doing it. Soon it'll be ours."

Vero slapped the bar with one hand. "Holy shit, girl—are you kidding me?"

"Not messing, not kidding. You happy?"

"Happy? Haven't been this excited since nasty cousin Herb fell face first into a pile of mud at the family reunion. This is cause for celebration."

Lola smiled harder. "Thanks, V."

"How'd you pull it off? This got something to do with that cousin of yours who died?"

"Great uncle," Lola corrected.

"Uncle? I could've sworn Johnny said…" She narrowed her eyes. A couple seconds passed. Lola's hands went clammy as Vero's expression morphed and she tilted her head back, shaking it. "No. Something's off here."

"Nothing is off. Seriously."

"Lola. Oh, fuck. What did you do?"

"Nothing—"

"You slept with that man." She tiptoed closer. "You *slept* with…? Oh, honey, I wasn't serious when I said—I didn't think you'd go through with it."

The room was too hot. Vero was too close. Lola hopelessly fanned herself with her hand. She'd never been a good liar. "It-it's complicated. Even if I thought I could explain, it wouldn't make any sense."

Vero looked across the room. "Johnny let you do this?"

"He didn't 'let' me do anything," Lola said. "We made a decision. Together."

"Hell, no." She shook her head like her mass of frizzy curls was on fire. "No, no, no. My man ever asked me to have sex with someone else, he'd see the business end of my fist before he got the words out. Don't matter how much money's involved."

"Vero," Lola said. "There's so much more to the situation than you think. Just let it be."

"Let it be? I can't. This is not cool."

"Johnny and I have been through hell these past few weeks," Lola said. "There's no way you could understand."

"What I understand is that you just took a very wrong turn down a dangerous path."

"Veronica," Lola said, shocked. "You're judging me? Have I ever *once* judged your choices? Didn't I support your decision to stay with Freddy after the way he treated you? Didn't Johnny and I take you in for weeks when you finally cut him loose?"

"That's different. That was between me and Freddy. But this isn't between you and Johnny because you brought a third person into your relationship, and now he'll never go away. Promise you that."

Lola frowned. It wasn't that Vero was necessarily wrong, but Lola couldn't handle her on top of Johnny on top of Hey Joe. She didn't need anyone to tell her what they'd done was wrong.

"What I need right now is a friend, Vero," Lola said.

Vero abruptly reached out and hugged Lola. Hard. It took Lola a moment to reciprocate. "You and I go back," Vero said softly. "When you came here, I thought you were just another chick. But knowing you has changed my life. You need me, I'm here."

"You're the one who changed mine," Lola said. "You and Johnny straightened me out."

Vero drew back a little to look Lola in the face. "Because it didn't take me long to see that you're better than this shit. And now I hear this." She shook her head sadly. "It's Johnny I'm pissed at, babe. Not you. But I'll keep it to myself because you asked me to. I'm just sorry you felt the need to do it. I-I hope it was, you know, worth it."

"It will be when we all get Hey Joe back to what it should be."

"If anyone can, it's you two. You'll survive this. Strong as an ox, girl."

Was she? Was Lola strong enough? She wasn't so sure. Now that they'd decided not to take Beau's offer, the weight of reality was growing heavier. Every hour she was in the bar, she thought of how soon it would all be theirs. It was more responsibility than she'd ever had in her life.

Vero finally let go of her. "What was it like?"

"With Beau?" Lola bit her bottom lip. "Like a wild dream stuck on fast forward. I think I went to another world for a few hours—like it wasn't even *real*."

Vero looked around the bar and held her palms face up toward the ceiling. "And now you guys get everything you wanted."

"Mostly," Lola said. "Turns out running a bar's expensive."

"I could've told you that. But we'll make this work. Even if I got to show up on time, I'm with you guys."

Lola half smiled. "Thanks. Means a lot."

Vero was suddenly even closer. "So, all right. We know it was fucked up, but sometimes that's the best kind. I bet that tall drink of water stripped off his designer suit to reveal all kinds of kinky. Tell me about the sex."

Lola blushed furiously, waving her off with a rag. "Stop it."

"That good?" Vero's eyes got big. "You *enjoyed* it?"

"Quiet," Lola said. "That's the last thing Johnny needs to hear."

"So you did," she stated as if that proved anything.

Lola looked at her hands. It hadn't been kinky to Lola. It'd been more natural, just—right. He'd done new things to her, like commanding her to her hands and knees, and she'd liked them. He'd done normal things and made them worthy of fireworks. The sixteenth floor of the Four Seasons was a private space for her to be completely herself and to experience Beau without guilt. "It was different," she said carefully. "Completely and utterly different than anything I've ever experienced." Lola looked up. "Just different."

"Lola. It's sex. It's okay if you enjoyed it. That's kind of what's supposed to happen."

"Let me put it this way. He's everything you'd think by looking at him and more."

"More?"

Lola thought immediately of his cock, how large it'd been in her hand, how it'd dominated her mouth. It wasn't what she'd meant, but she had a feeling Vero was thinking the same thing. "More. Sometimes it was like he knew me better than I knew myself. Like he'd memorized a map beforehand or something. And not just of my body. It—I can't really put it into words."

"I can. Basically he fucked your brains out."

Lola was done blushing. This time she tutted at Vero, but she said, "Right out of my head."

"Damn." Vero shrugged. "That's all I got, just—*damn*. He must've been something else."

"He was. Just don't mention any of this to Johnny."

"How's he taking it?"

"I'm not sure." Lola glanced over at her boyfriend. He was laughing with a table of customers she didn't recognize. He always made people feel at home. "He's been pretty quiet about it. I'm just glad he's getting all this."

"He'll do great, the bastard," Vero said. "Give it some time, though. Guess that's all you can do now. Don't overthink things."

Don't overthink things. Lola had tried to erase Beau's text message and his number. Each time, she hesitated until the screen went black. His number within reach— that felt like thinking about him. Like he was right there. Once she erased it, he would be gone. Officially.

When the bar was at its busiest a few hours later, Lola snuck out back for a cigarette. She'd assumed no one would notice, but Johnny opened the door a minute later. He looked around until he spotted her leaning against the building's brick wall.

"You all right?" he asked, coming over. "Been a while since you had one of those."

She nodded. "Are you?"

"I'm fine."

She offered him the cigarette, and he took a drag. "I've missed that," he said with his exhale.

"Tell me about it."

"Look at us," he said. "We're buying a business. We quit smoking. We're adults."

"When did that happen?"

"Fuck if I know. We had fun, though. Think we're still fun?"

"Fun adults? I think the two are mutually exclusive."

He smiled. "Yeah. Last week I told Tom if he opened the bar late one more time, I'd beat his ass. I'm my dad."

Lola laughed. "You even sound like him when you say it."

Johnny put the cigarette to his lips. He had that far off look in his eyes she'd been seeing too much of lately.

"What's going on, Johnny?" she asked. "Are you pissed at me?"

He looked down at her. "Pissed?"

"You're distant. You've barely talked to me all night."

"You were right the other day. I have to get serious about the bar now. I can't be screwing around anymore."

"That's not what I meant. This is a lot of work, but it's supposed to be fun too. This is a dream come true."

"Yeah. Just need a little time to get adjusted."

"You left home without me today," Lola said. "I had to hitch a ride with Vero."

"I had a meeting with Mitch."

Lola felt as if she'd been slapped. It had never once occurred to her that either of them would need to meet with Mitch alone. She leaned toward him. "You don't think maybe I ought to be there for that?"

"That's what you want, babe, sure. I thought I was supposed to handle the business stuff."

She proceeded with caution for both their sakes. Johnny's voice had an edge to it that she'd heard during their arguments, usually when he was too frustrated to remain rational. "I want this to be your baby," Lola said. "It's your dream. But I'm part of this too—a big part. You're in charge, but that doesn't mean I'm not at all in charge. I'm here to make decisions *and* to support you however I can."

He laughed just under his breath. "However you can. I'd say so."

"You know what? I don't like this snarky side of you." She'd probably said things she shouldn't have at some point too, but it wasn't in either of their natures to be deliberately mean.

He shrugged and looked up at the sky.

"Are you mad because I won't do it again?" she asked. "Or because I would?"

"Well, which is it?" he asked, his head still tilted back.

"Whatever you want it to be," Lola said.

"I just want the truth."

"And that's all I've ever wanted from you."

"All right, so give it to me straight." He glanced back down at her. "You want to or you don't? Did you enjoy yourself?"

"We agreed not to get into details."

"Jesus Christ." He laughed in disbelief. "No wonder you don't want me asking questions. You *did* enjoy it."

"Would you prefer I hated it? On my back, silently crying, pleading at the ceiling for it to be over?" She turned her face away as her cheeks got hot. It was almost as if he'd heard her conversation with Vero, but he'd been across the room.

The cigarette burned down in his hand, and he didn't respond.

She knew the answer to her own question. Things could've gone much worse with Beau, and she was grateful they hadn't. She'd do a lot for Johnny, but she wasn't going to wish it'd been terrible for her just so he would feel better. "I'd do it again," she said. "If you thought it was for the best."

"For the best," Johnny murmured. "The best being money."

"The best being our future."

"But here's the clincher, folks," he said. "The kind of future they want costs money."

"If you feel that strongly, just tell me not to do it."

"Thought we already decided you wouldn't." He tossed the cigarette on the ground and stamped it out. "You want to do it, then do it. Don't try to make it look like I'm asking you for it. You did it once, so it's not even like it's that big of a deal."

Lola set her jaw. "How can you say that?"

He walked away. "You got his number," he said, pulling open the back door. "You don't need me to make the arrangements."

Lola stared after him. She had the strange but satisfying sense that she'd gotten away with something. Like she'd get as a young girl when her mom would occasionally let her pick one thing from the candy aisle. But it was more than that. Johnny wouldn't make a firm decision, so she had to, and if he came to regret the outcome, he'd only have himself to blame for not speaking up. She was free to make the mistake that— she was slowly figuring out—she wanted to make.

She hadn't stopped thinking about the way Beau had owned her, as if it were a craving she couldn't kick. Beau's unwavering attention—the only kind he knew— could easily become addicting.

She took out another cigarette to calm herself—her hand shook as she lit it. Money? What money? It was becoming less important the greater her need grew. Not just any kind of need, but the kind Beau incited in her, that built and built to an unbearable level. The kind only he could fulfill. She was feeling that way more and more lately, whenever she thought of him like she did now.

And now she'd get her fix again. The decision was made for her. Johnny had cemented it when he'd walked away. She took her cell from her pocket and pulled up Beau's phone number.

"Lola, ma chatte," Beau answered. His voice was low and raw.

"You were sleeping," she said.

"It's one in the morning."

"I'm sorry."

"Don't be," he said. "Unless this is a dream. Then you should be very sorry."

She smiled. Except for a yellow streetlamp nearby, it was dark. They were alone.

"How are you?" he asked.

She blew out a breath and flicked ash from her cigarette. "I'm okay."

"Most women who call me in the middle of the night are not okay."

"I don't want to be most women," Lola said quietly.

"You aren't. Not to me."

She closed her eyes. "I wish you wouldn't say things like that."

"So this call isn't personal, then. That would make it business."

Lola waited. Her mind was even more made up hearing his voice, but she couldn't sound too eager. Just like Johnny, Beau had to know with certainty that money anchored their arrangement. That there were boundaries. "What are the terms of your new offer?"

After rustling on the other end and a short silence, he said, "The same. Including the test if you've slept with Johnny again."

"Why would that matter?"

"If you've had a partner after the test, then it matters."

There was that sterile word again—*partner*. "Beau, he's my boyfriend."

"You weren't with him the night you were with me. Who knows how he kept himself occupied?"

She stared daggers at the back door. She knew Johnny better than she knew anyone, and he wasn't a cheater. "Johnny would never. You don't know him."

"I don't have to. I know people. Resentment is ugly. It makes people do ugly things."

She shook her head. "He wouldn't."

"So have you slept with him?"

She took a drag of her cigarette. She imagined Beau sitting forward in his bed, the sheet around his lap. The corner of his hungry mouth twitching as he waited. His mouth was so goddamn hungry when it was on her. "No. Have you?"

"He's not my type."

"Be serious. You know what I mean."

"I haven't seen anyone. The impression you left is…unshakeable."

"How romantic," she said dryly to hide the fact that she wanted it to be true.

"You asked me to be serious. I am. Housekeeping has replaced the sheets but I smell your perfume here. It's impossible, I know." His voice dropped even lower. "The window is still smudged from your tits."

Her pulse stuttered. From the start, he'd been catching her off guard, startling her with his brashness. She bit her lip, knowing any noise she made would come out sounding like a moan. "I—I don't wear perfume."

He chuckled. "So, Lola. Do we have a deal?"

"Five hundred the night before. Five hundred the next morning."

"Sunset to sunrise."

"When?" she asked.

"If I hadn't already lost the hours, I'd say right now. God knows I want you here. Can it be tomorrow?"

"It's a weekday."

"But you work nights," he said. "You can sleep the next day."

"I meant for you."

"Don't worry about me. My impatience reaches disconcerting levels where you're involved."

"I'm flattered. I think." She hesitated, not ready to get off the phone. Talking to him was smoothing out the rollercoaster week she'd had, a temporary cure for her distress. "Tomorrow."

"Tomorrow," he repeated.

She hung up before she said something she shouldn't—like "I can't wait" or "I look forward to having you inside me again." The stab of guilt in her gut was drowned by the quick beats of her heart. Vero and Johnny were both right. Lola liked this. She enjoyed it. Not only that—she fucking *wanted* it.

Chapter Five

Lola couldn't come up with the words to tell him. She and Johnny had been driving home from the bar for ten minutes, but she'd been pretending to sleep with her head back against the passenger seat headrest. In fact, she'd been awake, searching for those impossible words to say she'd promised herself to another man tomorrow night. It was hard enough without wondering if Johnny would be relieved or angry. Was *she* relieved? Was she angry? Johnny wasn't acting like the man she knew he was. It made her wonder if he'd ever been, or if it was possible she'd built him up to something else over the years.

Johnny pulled into their parking spot and shut off the car. "When we own the bar, does that mean we can hire other people to work this late?"

She looked over at him. It was the first attempt at conversation he'd made since their argument.

"We're getting too old for this shit," he continued. There was something in his voice—nerves? Guilt? When she didn't respond, he said, "I'm sorry about earlier. I acted like a jerk."

Lola glanced at her hands. "I'm not admitting to that. To the thing about being too old." One thing she appreciated about Johnny was his ability to admit his faults. When they fought, he almost always apologized first. And when he didn't, it was because he didn't think he'd done anything wrong. "I promised my early-twenties self that I'd never get old," she said. "But my late-twenties self is having a tough time holding up her end of the bargain."

Johnny grinned—she knew without even looking. Things were right with him again, but not for long. As they got out of the car and walked to their apartment, the air around Lola seemed thick, as if a storm were brewing.

Johnny fought with the lock on the front door. "Every damn time," he muttered. He flipped on the lights once they were inside. "We should think about getting a new place."

"I'd like that," Lola said.

He tossed his keys on the coffee table. "How much would you love not paying rent?"

"So much," she said on the way to the kitchen. "Adults pay mortgages, after all."

"Yep." He came up behind her, curling his arms around her middle as she poured herself water from the tap. "You know what else adults do?"

"I can think of a thing or two," she said.

He nuzzled her neck, squeezing her to him. "How about a shower to wash the night off? We both stink like cigarettes." He slid his hands up to her breasts. "Good thing I like you anyway."

"A shower at three in the morning?"

"I don't care. Horny, babe."

Water flooded the glass in the sink. She was unaffected by his advances. His cruelty and abrupt dismissal earlier still left her chilly. But even if she responded to Johnny's touch, she couldn't sleep with him. Not after she'd told Beau she hadn't.

"Johnny," she said.

"Yeah."

"I called him."

He stopped moving. His breath warmed her cheek. Her anxious heart was trying to burst out of her chest.

"What?" He released her. "You're going back?"

She turned around and steeled herself against the sink. "Yes."

"But you—I thought we'd discuss it more."

"You said what you had to say outside the bar. I didn't like it, but you said it. So I made the call."

"Well, fuck." He ran his hands over his scalp and held them up. "You just made the call, that's it?"

"He agreed to another million," she said. "Same terms as before."

He dropped his arms at his sides. "You should've discussed this with me. What if I didn't want you to do it again? Or what if we could've gotten more? We hold the cards here."

She gripped the counter, narrowing her eyes. The money was becoming too important a factor for him. "Don't be ridiculous. Another million is more than enough. And you're the one who told me to call."

"Come on, Lola. You know how I am. I was mouthing off because I was pissed."

She'd known exactly that, but she'd made the call anyway. Did that mean she was to blame? "So, what? You don't want me to do it?"

He blew his cheeks out with his exhale. "I…"

They both looked away from each other, he into the next room and she at the stove. Her heartbeat had slowed. There was no point in pretending he didn't want that money enough to let her do this again. She wasn't the only bad guy. Her desire to see Beau became less of a weight on her shoulders.

"I saw a video online. You and him at that benefit or whatever." Johnny's eyes darted over the floor.

"When?"

"A couple days ago."

She'd forgotten he might see that. Johnny'd wanted details—how was that for one? Her red lips glued to Beau's mouth, turning his lips red too? "Why didn't you tell me?"

He shrugged in his lumbering way, looking up again. "Brenda found it on one of those entertainment news sites. Mark showed me it on his phone."

"What'd you say?"

"It caught me totally off guard," he said. "I had nothing."

Her stomach heaved. She covered it with one arm. Mark and Brenda weren't judgmental people, but that didn't matter. A situation like this was nearly impossible to justify. "You told them the truth? Please tell me you're joking."

"What was I supposed to say, it was your long lost twin out for a night on the town with one of the richest men in Los Angeles? Mark and I played pool with the guy the night he came into the bar."

"Too many people know."

"You should've thought of that. Did you not notice the cameras? I asked you not to kiss him, so you went and did it in front of thousands of people."

"But, Johnny, he—"

"Yeah, yeah, he made you do it. They called you 'Beau Olivier's Sassy Mystery Woman.' *Sassy*? In what universe do people use that word? And to describe *my* girlfriend?"

"You don't understand. I was playing a part."

"You were damn convincing too. Especially when you told that reporter to take her hands off your man. Real *sassy*. You think I liked having to watch that in front of my best friend? Trying not to react?"

Lola rubbed under her eyes with her knuckles. "I'm sorry you had to see that, but you know what I was dealing with."

"Whatever." He started to leave, but turned back to her. His stance relaxed, and he put his hands out, as if asking her for help with something. It reminded her of the first time he'd come with her to the Laundromat, and she'd explained the concept of delicates. "So tell me how this goes," he said. "He picks you up. Takes you—where, his place? A motel? Does he push you onto your knees or do you go willingly?"

She flinched. "Stop it."

"In your stupid dress and red lipstick—yeah, I saw that on the video too. Why don't you wear lipstick like that for me?"

"Like what?" she asked. "You want me to wear red lipstick while I wait tables at a dive bar?"

"Did it ever occur to you that I might like to see you in such a fancy dress?"

"No, because it's not us. That was some girl Beau dressed up like a doll."

"Oh, drop the act. What girl wouldn't love to be fussed over like that?"

So what if she had? The hair on the back of her neck rose. "You want me to dress up for you, then maybe you could make a fucking fuss over me once in a while."

His eyebrows shot up. "You think I don't? I brag about you to anyone who'll listen. My hot-as-shit girlfriend Lola—have you seen her in leather pants? Do you know how smart she is, how many ideas she has? Have you seen those eyes? I love those fucking blue eyes, man." Johnny leaned his hands against the tiled counter and took a deep breath. "I'm the luckiest son of a *fucking* bitch."

Johnny had his moments, but hearing how highly he thought of her was harrowing. It was almost enough for her to confess her attraction to Beau so it would stop feeling like such a secret between them. But she couldn't bring herself to. She'd already imagined Beau at the curb several times, waiting for her to come to him. It *was* a secret, and it was dirty.

If she didn't go now, her mind would fill in the blanks of their night together. Driving somewhere exciting to start the night. Beau, unable to keep his hands off her in public knowing how good it could be.

"We can't do this," Johnny said.

Lola jerked her head to him. But she'd made the decision for them both. He'd had his chance. He didn't get to say no now. Did he? She couldn't cancel. She didn't want to.

"We can't fight," he continued. "If we don't go into this together, then you're going in alone, and that puts us on opposite sides. With him in middle. We can't let him get between us."

Divided they were weaker. Beau knew that too, though. Her connection with Johnny stretched thinner the more it was pulled in opposite directions.

"We've done this once already, so how do we do it better this time?" He pushed off the counter and paced in front of her. He pulled on his chin. "It's like this. B— no, not business. Logical. This plus this equals that. Remove the emotional side and look at it logically. I'm not so good at that, babe, but you are. And I can try."

"Logical?" she asked. There was nothing logical about her and Beau in the same room, but there could be between her and Johnny. She followed him with her eyes.

"You already know what to expect," he said. "It was, what, less than twelve hours? For a million bucks." He paused. "He didn't hurt you. He didn't force you."

She shook her head.

"Say something."

It couldn't be done. Beau couldn't be managed. But Lola already felt him. She already tasted him. He was too close for her to walk away now. So she said, "I think you might be right."

"Two million gets us everything we wanted for the bar plus a new place and a car for you. Wouldn't that be enough?" he asked.

"Yes. It'll leave us a decent amount."

"Good." He nodded.

"But this is where we draw the line," she said. "I don't care if it's ten million for a week. This is far enough for me." No matter how tempted she was to spend more time with Beau, he'd bought enough of her. This had to be the last night for them.

Johnny stopped walking and came to stand in front of her. He cupped her face. "It is. This will be enough." His hands twitched like he was going to let go, but he didn't. "You know what else this gets us?"

"What?"

"A wedding fund."

Lola bit her lip. "Johnny."

"And a college fund."

It was the worst moment to bring up marriage and kids. It blended her budding desire for those things, her guilt over wanting Beau and her disappointment in

Johnny—and herself—into the same pot. She pressed her hand to her chest. "Are you…you're serious?"

"Thought I was a piece of shit for wanting to bring a kid into the world when I had nothing to give him. But now? Everything's different. Send him to fucking Harvard if I want."

Lola hadn't even known where Harvard was until a few years ago. She couldn't keep up with what Johnny was saying. While she was selling her body for their future, there was no space in her mind for what that bought her. The picture wouldn't form.

Everything teetered dangerously close to the edge. She wasn't sure if the right decision was to reach out and pull it back—or to let it fall.

Chapter Six

When Lola was fourteen, she'd stolen makeup from a nearby drugstore. Some crimes were small. Some were big. Some were never found out—like the makeup— and then, were they really crimes at all? Lola paced in front of the window, pausing every few minutes to see the sun a little lower. She didn't even need what she'd taken. For years, she'd walked an extra four blocks to a different drugstore.

Lola stopped her march to watch the building across the street eat the last sliver of sun. Almost right away, a black limo appeared through the complex gate.

By the way her palms sweat and her heart pounded like they had fifteen years ago, Lola knew instinctively— she shouldn't get in that limo. There was more at stake than Johnny realized. Maybe enough to change them permanently. What kind of crime was it to do it anyway? If nobody knew but her, did it matter?

Beau had sent over a large box earlier that day with a red bow around it. The gift was lavish—a gold, beaded dress that crisscrossed in the back and had one slit all the way to her upper right thigh. Johnny had played it off—Beau had to pay for Lola's attention, and Johnny got that for free. But Lola had ignored him, running her fingers over the intricate beadwork. She didn't need to be pampered or spoiled, but that didn't mean it wasn't nice once in a while.

Lola had waited to change until Johnny'd left for work. She'd done her makeup, attempting to recreate her look from her first evening with Beau so he'd look at her again the way he had in the reflection of the salon's mirror. This time, though, she left her hair down.

Lola opened the door before Warner had a chance to knock. "Good evening, Miss Winters. Mr. Olivier is ready for you."

She locked the apartment behind her. "How long have you worked for Beau?" she asked as they curved around the pool and crossed the courtyard.

Warner kept his eyes forward. "Almost ten years."

"You must've been young when you started."

"Only a few years older than Mr. Olivier."

"Have you always wanted to—drive? Do you do other things?"

"I also drive Miss Leroux."

"Who?"

He leaned forward and opened the limo door. Beau had a pile of papers on his lap and a phone to his ear. He nodded at her and covered the mouthpiece. "Wait there a moment." He returned to his conversation as Lola stood on the sidewalk. Warner had disappeared.

Beau hung up without even a goodbye. He made a note on the paperwork in his lap, then tossed it on the car floor. He smiled up at her—like he was a king who'd just returned from a long day ruling his kingdom and had found her waiting for him. He got out of the car.

"What are you doing?" she asked.

He stood up to his full height and looked down on her. He lifted her chin with his knuckle, and just that one point of contact covered her in goose bumps. She'd selected her highest heels for the evening, but her head still tilted back for Beau.

"Thank you for dressing the part tonight," he said. "Though you were stunning in old jeans, something this beautiful finally does you justice."

He was sincere. The compliments he paid her never seemed to serve as a means to get something, even a reaction. It made her uncharacteristically weak in the knees.

"Any credit goes to the dress," she said. "Thank you for sending it."

Neither of them looked away. There were memories in the way they took from each other's eyes. For Lola, it was the way she fit into his arms as they fell asleep. It was the way he fucked her like he owned her.

"Let's go inside."

She took an automatic step back, blinking everything between them away. "Inside?" she asked, touching her chin where he'd just touched her. "What?"

"I'd like to see your place."

"No."

"No?" His tone was reminder enough that no matter what moments they'd had, he was in charge.

She panicked and blurted the first thing that came to her. "We can't. Johnny's home."

"I don't believe you. Last time he watched from the window."

She hadn't known that. She glanced over her shoulder. "Well, okay, you're right—he's...he's at work, but—"

"He didn't stay to see you off?" Beau asked, tilting his head.

"We decided it was better this way. The whole emotional goodbye thing was hard last time."

"So then it shouldn't be a problem. If you don't want him to know, don't tell him." He took a step, but she moved into his path.

"Why?" she asked.

He shrugged. "I want a glimpse into your life. It will help complete the picture in my head."

Her apartment was the last piece of her and Johnny Beau hadn't infiltrated. It was Johnny's kingdom, but she worried Beau would make it his the moment he walked in. "I'm not comfortable with that."

Beau made a point of turning and squinting at the sky behind him. It was still light out, but the sun was gone. He looked back at Lola. "Should we review the terms of our agreement?"

Sweat coated her upper lip. She licked it away. "No. That won't be necessary."

He inclined forward as if to kiss her and stopped. He'd taken his time the first night to make sure she was comfortable, but they were past that now. Did he need an invitation? She resisted the urge to lick her lips a second time.

He turned away to take something from the car and close the door. "Go ahead, ma chatte. Lead the way."

She went back the way she'd just come, Beau close behind her. Despite her wariness of his request, her body thrummed being with him again. She jiggled the key a few times until the lock gave and cleared her throat. "It's stubborn."

Beau walked into the apartment with one hand in his pocket. Under his arm was a medium-sized package wrapped in brown craft paper. Another present? It was uncomfortable, him spending money on her when he'd paid so much for one evening. He'd already given her the dress, and whatever plans they had tonight that warranted such a gown wouldn't come cheap.

He glanced up at the ceiling, then at a pillow on the couch. Johnny'd slept there the night before since he'd been unusually restless and hadn't wanted to keep Lola awake. Beau wandered across the room and looked down the hallway toward their bedroom.

"I wasn't expecting company," Lola said, picking up Johnny's dishes from the coffee table. She carried them to the sink.

Beau found her in the kitchen. "I like seeing people in their natural states. Don't clean on my account." He walked to the fridge and pulled a photo from under a magnet. "Camping?"

"In Yosemite."

He studied Johnny and Lola's smiling faces. "You have freckles."

"They're more noticeable when I get sun."

"You look young," he said. "And happy."

"We were."

He looked up at her with one eyebrow arched.

"Young, I mean," she said. "We *were* young. We're still happy."

His thumb pressed into the corner, sending a wrinkle through the center. He dumped the package heavily on the kitchen counter. "That's the first half of the money. I brought it in cash this time to avoid unwanted attention."

"Oh." She stared at the parcel, feeling foolish. It'd been presumptuous to assume it was a gift. "Maybe I should put it in a closet or something."

"That would be wise."

Before she could move, he dropped the photo on top of the money and walked over to her. She held up her hands to stop him, but he took her face and kissed her, backing her against the counter.

She shoved him off. "Stop," she said, panting. "This is his home."

He looked into her eyes. "That's the last time tonight I'll allow you to push me away. I've been as patient as I can." He was also breathing hard. "Since we said goodbye, you're all I've thought of."

"You wanted to see my place, fine. As long as we're here, though, I'm off limits. Completely. I don't give a damn about our agreement."

He continued to stare at her. She braced herself, knowing how touchy he could be when it came to Johnny. Instead, he took a step back. "Then we'd better go. I'm having a hard time getting ahold of myself."

They made their way outside, and she locked up. Had he said he'd been thinking of her since they'd said goodbye?

On the way to the car, he took her hand and brought it to his lips. "I'm glad you called. What we discussed on the phone—it still stands, doesn't it?"

"I haven't been with Johnny."

"I can't say I'm surprised."

He was baiting her, but she didn't even want to know what he'd meant by that. She looked at the ground. Did Beau think Johnny would be repulsed by her? Or that Lola was the one who didn't want it? She took the bait. "Why aren't you surprised?"

"I challenge any man to be okay with knowing the woman he loves was just with someone else. Not just the act of it, but the intimacy. The closeness. The touching, whispering." He glanced over at her, narrowing his eyes a fraction. "I'm not okay with it. Far from it."

His voice was almost accusatory, as if he were in Johnny's shoes. "Are you talking about him or yourself? Does it bother you, Johnny and me?"

He returned his eyes forward as they approached the car, and it was a moment before he answered. He leaned over to open the door for her. "Yes."

She didn't move. "But I'm not the woman you love."

73

He remained passive except that the angles of his jaw sharpened. "Just imagine if you were."

Chapter Seven

Within seconds of pulling away from the curb of Lola's apartment complex, Beau placed his hand just inside the slit of her dress and squeezed gently. She didn't expect his touch to overwhelm her like it did, as if it were the eye of a hurricane, the spot the rest of her body revolved around. She grabbed his wrist and pulled him off.

"What's wrong?" His cheek dimpled at one corner of his mouth.

"It's too much," she said.

"But it's nothing."

"It should be."

He replaced his hand but this time slid it under the dress. "You say you're doing this for the money. Maybe that's what he needs to hear. Your body tells a different story, though." His fingers edged along the inside of her thigh. "I know the other night's played a loop in your thoughts, just like it has in mine."

She shored up her resolve. Beau no doubt expected her to give in completely, but it was early. It was his nature to push, and it was hers to push back. She was having a hard time remembering why she should, though, with his hand burning against her skin. "Where are you taking me tonight?" she asked to change the subject.

"Care to take a guess?"

"In this gown, somewhere fancier than I've ever been. Right?"

"I don't know where you've been." He was teasing her, mischief in his twinkling eyes.

She pressed her lips together to suppress a smile. "There's a movie premiere in Hollywood."

"Not that unusual."

She shifted in her seat. "And the L.A. Opera season opened this week. *La Traviata* is playing."

"You've given this some thought."

"I looked online." Lola didn't want to sound overeager, but she'd been wondering all afternoon what was in store. "Of course, it's L.A.—there're tons of things happening. But those both sounded exciting."

He smiled. "Our first stop is to see my sister in the Hollywood Hills. It won't take five minutes."

Lola's brows furrowed. While researching Beau, she hadn't read anything about siblings. "You never mentioned a sister. Is she younger or older?"

"Younger by a couple years. You can wait in the car if you'd like."

She feigned interest in her fingernails. "Yes, that's probably best."

After a brief silence, he said, "Or, you can meet her. I'd like that."

She glanced up. "Wouldn't that be weird?"

"Not for me. Brigitte and I often attend the same events, so she's met some of my dates."

"Were they also paid to stand by your side, though?"

Beau looked as though he'd bitten into a lemon. "Of course not. You don't have to give her all the details."

"Right," she said. "I guess that would be fine."

"Good." He rubbed her leg. "I like that you wore the dress," he said softly. "I like that you shaved your legs again. Even if it wasn't for me."

His hand moved over her skin as though they'd never parted. Their connection hadn't weakened with time apart. She was just as hungry for his hand to move higher—to give her what only he could. She was supposed to be pushing back, but his pull was strong.

"It was," she said.

She was there, somewhere she both did and did not want to be. She could fight—he would win. She could give everything over—he would demand more. There was a war in and outside of her. Her against herself. Her against him. His weapons were growing, even as she inched over to his side.

He moved a little closer. His stiff hair smelled of men's product. She reached up and took a piece that had separated and fallen over his forehead. She slid her fingers along it to put it in place, but it just swung back. He had touched her—her chin, her leg, his lips to hers, his hand around hers, but she had not yet touched him except for that strand of hair. She wanted more. Wasn't it okay to take it? Isn't that what all three parties involved had agreed to?

This was her life for the next however many hours, and in that moment, she didn't feel like pretending she hated it. "Beau."

"Lola."

"Roll up the partition."

He swallowed audibly. "We're almost there."

She leaned over and hit the button herself. "This won't take long," she whispered. She thought her advance would've surprised him, but no sooner had she lifted a knee than he was pulling her onto his lap. He released her to unbutton his slacks, but she stopped him.

"Let me," she said.

She moved his hands to her breasts. He felt her impatiently, his fingers so hard she winced. She took him out. He went to put his mouth on her nipple, but she caught his face and lifted it to hers. "There's no time for that," she said. Her mouth pulled to his like a magnet to steel. They kissed with the same fury of urgency. She pushed aside her underwear and helped him inside her, taking a few agonizingly long moments to adjust to his girth when all she wanted was to screw him fast.

They began to move. She took his earlobe in her mouth as they found their rhythm. His fingers dug into her scalp, skin—anywhere he could get.

He took over, securing her hips to him and thrusting up into her. Her head fell back. The car ceiling blurred with bright spots. He guided her with one hand and circled her clit with the other. The ache from the last few days balled low in her stomach, growing and growing until she gasped in a silent scream with the crest of her orgasm. Beau pulled her off of him. He took himself in one hand, held her hip with the other and came all over the insides of her thighs.

"Beau," she panted. "God, Beau. How? How are we so…?"

His breaths were also labored. "Fast?"

She was going to say "good together," but even in her state, she knew she shouldn't. He looked at her as if he knew anyway.

They were no longer driving. Beau searched the space around them and scratched the back of his head. He frowned. "I didn't plan for sex in the car."

"I apologize for the disruption to tonight's program," she said, her mouth tingling with the urge to smile.

"It's all right," he said distractedly. "I just—aha." He picked her up and moved her from his lap to the seat. He reached for a beverage napkin from the limo's built-in bar, pulled her leg open and wiped the inside of one thigh.

"What are you doing?" she asked.

"Cleaning you."

It was unnecessary, but she didn't stop him. Being felt that way only added to the warm satisfaction her orgasm had left her with. "Why'd you pull out?" she asked.

His eyes traveled up. They glinted to match his smirk. "My sister can be intense. Your concentration should be on her at all times. I didn't want to leave anything behind that might—distract you."

"Oh. Always one step ahead," she murmured.

He dropped the napkin but didn't stop touching her.

Lola's head fell back against the window. "Your hands feel good."

"You mean when they aren't trying to get in your underwear?"

"That too." She smiled. "But this is also nice."

He pressed his thumbs to the insides of her thighs and massaged. "You keep tensing. Are you nervous?"

"No," she said, her eyes closed. "You have strong hands. And I'm not used to this."

"To what?"

"A massage. I haven't had many in my life."

He stopped. "You haven't?"

She lifted her head to look at him. "Our definitions of luxury are probably a little different. For instance, a car wash is something I only allow when we're flush."

"Oh, no." He crawled over her body and kissed her. "Tonight." He pecked her again. "You're getting the massage of your life."

"From you?" she asked.

"As if I want anyone else touching you."

The window rattled suddenly, and they jumped away from each other like teenagers caught making out.

"Beau?" came a woman's voice. She peered through the glass.

"Don't worry," he said as he tucked himself back into his pants. "They're tinted."

Lola fixed her underwear and dress. Instinctively, she leaned over and straightened Beau's tie. It was red, like the one he'd been wearing the night they'd met.

Before she could move away, he put his hand around her wrist and pulled her back. "Thanks," he said, kissing her once. "If I haven't said it yet, thank you for saying yes. I love—having you by my side."

He unlocked the door and got out while Lola stayed frozen where she was. He'd stumbled over the word *love* as if he were going to say something else. Something like "I love *you*." Her—*Lola*, which was ridiculous. True, from the moment they'd met, their relationship had been intense. Their first night had been a series of dates in the span of a few hours. They had a connection—an *attraction*—but it didn't matter. It couldn't evolve beyond the physical.

"You've been sitting at the curb for ten minutes," she heard from outside in a woman's noticeable French accent. "What the hell were you doing?"

Beau cleared his throat. "Business call."

"Business?" She eyed Lola as she exited the car behind him. "Of course. Yes."

Lola found herself face to face with a woman who looked nothing like Beau. Her raven-colored hair was wrapped into a chignon. She just came up to Lola's chin, and she seemed to know it, turning her thin, pointed nose up in the air for added height.

Lola extended her hand and introduced herself.

His sister waved at the air around them. "I'm sure I'm coming down with something," she said. "I'd hate to get you sick."

Beau took Lola's hand instead and brought it to his side. "Lola, this is Brigitte. Who apparently has plans tonight."

Brigitte sighed and smoothed her hands over her tight, red sleeveless dress. "I don't, but my mother loved to say 'always dress for company.'"

"We're hardly company," Beau said.

"Good evening, Miss Leroux," Warner said from over the top of the limo.

"Ah," Brigitte said, "but Warner is here. Is he not worthy of such a beautiful dress?"

She trotted in her heels around the car to throw herself in Warner's open arms.

"Ignore her," Beau said to Lola, rolling his eyes. "She's that way with anyone who gives her attention. Warner took her to an event last week, yet she acts like he's just returned home from war." Brigitte stroked Warner's suited arm, threw her head back and laughed. Warner looked stunned by her—and Lola had to admit, she was stunning. He smiled so hard his cheeks turned red.

"We don't have much time," Beau interrupted their moment. "No time at all, actually."

"You're always rushing me," Brigitte said, turning her back on Warner without so much as a glance. She led the way up the sidewalk. "Is this the girl?"

"Brigitte," Beau warned.

"What girl?" Lola asked. She followed Beau into the house through a front door twice as tall as them.

"Don't be shy, brother." Brigitte looked over her shoulder at Lola. The ordinary brown of her eyes should've been comforting, yet they were far too sharp for that. "It's just that Beau rarely mentions anyone, except that he's been talking about this one girl…"

Beau inhaled a deep breath and closed his eyes a moment. "*Brigitte, sois sage.* Is Louis in the study?" He looked at Lola. "Our lawyer."

Lola's attention was drawn up to the entryway's chandelier. "Wow."

"Ah, yes. It's called a *Montgolfier*—after the brothers," Brigitte said. "Do you know them? They're French."

Lola shook her head.

"They only invented the hot air balloon. That's why it's shaped like one but upside down."

"It's lovely," Lola said, "just like your home." Her heels, shorter than Brigitte's, clicked on the foyer's marble floor.

"Technically it's Beau's," Brigitte said. "He lets me stay here."

"It's *our* home," Beau said to her. "I think after nearly a decade here, it's okay to say."

"I just hate for you to think I'm taking advantage." She looked at Lola. "Beau must be careful about that sort of thing."

Lola didn't want to go down that road. She slid her hand from Beau's. "I don't understand. You live here?"

"Yes," Brigitte answered.

Just moments ago, Lola had been thinking how well they knew each other for such a short time. She must not have known much if she didn't even know where he lived. It hit her that maybe he wanted it that way. Why else would he bring her to a hotel when he had a home nearby?

Lola turned away to avoid Beau's inquisitive look. The pearl-colored living room had matching drapes that framed long, French doors. Gold molding trimmed the room, complementing the gold accents in the lamps, vases and side tables. The walls were lined with simple, elegant artwork that continued into the hallways and up the spiral staircase. A large vase of white and purple Calla lilies sat center on the entryway table.

She'd done a complete turn and now found Brigitte with her arms surrounding Beau's neck. Her eyes were large with admiration for him, and there was lip-gloss grease on his cheek. "Did you miss your baby sister?" she asked.

"Come on, Brigitte," he said. "I saw you two days ago. Let me go check with Louis."

She dropped her arms with a huff. "Yes, he's in the study. I'll keep Lily company."

"Lola," he corrected.

"Right."

Beau leaned over and kissed Lola's cheek. "Will you be all right?"

She nodded. "Go ahead."

"A few minutes, ma chatte."

Brigitte scoffed just loud enough to be heard.

He ignored her, winking at Lola before disappearing behind double doors.

Brigitte turned to her. "So, have you known my brother long?"

"A couple weeks."

"Oh. That *is* long."

Lola smiled thinly. "Not for most people."

"Beau isn't most people. But I'm sure you've figured that out."

"I have," Lola said. "He's certainly unlike anyone I've ever met."

"Don't worry if you're flustered by him. That's normal. My brother isn't easy to read unless you know him like I do." She arched one thin, black eyebrow and looked from Lola's feet to her face. "You, on the other hand, I'm not so sure."

"Sorry?"

"My brother's money gets many admirers. He has a good nose for bullshit, except when it comes to particularly studied actresses. That's where he needs my help."

Lola crossed her arms. "That isn't me."

"No?"

"No. And my relationship with Beau isn't anyone's business but ours. He knows exactly what I want from him."

Brigitte circled Lola, watching her the entire time. "You aren't Beau's usual type."

"If you're trying to intimidate me, it won't work."

Brigitte came to a stop in front of her. "My, my. You truly aren't his type." Her knuckles brushed along Lola's arm. "I can see why he's attracted to you."

Lola glanced at Brigitte's hand and smiled faintly. "Are you coming on to me, Brigitte?"

"If it's money you're after, I'm no pauper myself."

"As if you have the slightest clue what I'm after."

Brigitte cooed and fluttered like a little bird. "I see you're not worried about making a good impression on me."

"I have no delusions about my relationship with Beau. It's temporary, and he knows that. Therefore I have no reason to impress you."

"Temporary," Brigitte repeated. "You flinched at the word."

Lola had hoped Brigitte wouldn't catch that. She narrowed her eyes. "And *you* have a vivid imagination."

"Do you love him?" she asked.

The question flustered Lola, but this time she was ready for it. Her face remained smooth. "If I do or don't, it isn't your business. You aren't your brother's keeper—or are you?"

Brigitte's eye twitched noticeably. "What was that he called you? Ma chatte?" She said the endearment so sharply, venom might've sprayed off her tongue. "Do you even know what it means?"

"His cat," Lola answered.

"Close. More like *his pussy*," Brigitte said.

Lola leaned in. "Well, it is."

"I can smell him on you."

"That's because we fucked on the way over."

Brigitte's lips paled with a tight smile. "Beau," she called loudly over Lola's shoulder. "We're finished here."

The door opened. "So are we," Beau said from behind Lola. "We'll be on our way then."

"See you tomorrow night," Brigitte said to him. "And goodbye, Lola." She didn't walk them out.

"Was she hard on you?" Beau asked on the way to the limo.

"I can handle her."

"I wouldn't have left you alone if I didn't believe that."

Warner already had the door open for them.

"She seems oddly protective," Lola noted.

"She's not actually my sister," Beau said.

Warner sniffed. He shut the door once they were inside.

"I shouldn't be surprised," Lola said. "You neither look nor sound anything alike."

Beau tugged on the end of his sleeve. "Would you like a drink?"

"No."

Lola waited as he fiddled with his cufflink. His brows got heavy, as if it required great concentration. Finally he said, "I don't talk about my family often. I prefer to keep my personal affairs—well, private."

It'd taken Lola a few months to introduce Johnny to her mother. She loved them both, but they represented two different things for her—her past and her future. Johnny and Dina now got along better than

Lola and Dina. "I understand," Lola said. "We can talk about something else."

"No, I…" He looked up and cleared his throat. "I want to tell you. It's part of who I am, and I want you to know me."

It was a step in a different direction for them—forward or backward, Lola wasn't sure, but she'd always been curious about this side of Beau, especially right after his proposition.

"I told you when I was seventeen I went to Paris with my dad for the summer. The trip was cut short because of his car accident. That's how he died."

Lola covered her mouth. "While you were there?"

"Yes. And he wasn't alone. He was with a woman he'd introduced me to as a friend earlier that summer—but as it turned out, they'd been having an affair for years. She was also killed."

"You didn't know about her?"

Beau shook his head slowly. "I had no idea. When I met her, she offered for her daughter, Brigitte, to show me around Paris since I didn't know anyone my own age. Brigitte and I became friends." He brushed his hand over his pants. The leather seat creaked as he shifted. "I found out later she knew the truth about our parents but didn't tell me. If I'd known, I would've stood up to him. For my mom."

There was irony in this information, considering how Beau was coming between Lola and Johnny. But maybe the two events were somehow related. Lola didn't mention it. Beau was clearly outside his comfort zone, and she didn't want him to clam up. "How'd Brigitte end up here?"

"She was born here, so she had dual citizenship even though she grew up there. She begged me to bring her back to America with me."

"But you'd only just met. Why would she want that?"

"She just felt...alone. Nowhere to turn." He pulled a little at his collar. "Imagine explaining to my mom about the fifteen-year-old girl I got off the plane with."

"She took in her husband's lover's kid?"

"Yes, and she didn't deal well with it. His death and finding out about the affair sent her into a deep depression that lasted almost two years. I had just finished high school, but I couldn't leave her like that so I lived with them. Then one day she was fine again."

"Just like that? What changed?"

"She was better for about six months. She lost weight, bought new clothes, cooked us lavish meals. She even took a trip. I moved out and Brigitte was getting ready to graduate. Everything was great."

"Until?"

"Until...we realized why she'd been so happy. As Brigitte's guardian, my mom was in charge of her inheritance—and in those six months, she'd spent all of it."

Lola's mouth fell open. "You're kidding."

"She tried to tell me we deserved that money more than Brigitte. And she's convinced Brigitte uses me for my money as revenge against her."

"Does she?"

"No. My mother has an active imagination."

"What makes you so sure?"

Beau frowned. "Brigitte and I lived together for a long time before I made even a dime. Brigitte was there through all of it, for every late night. When I couldn't see straight anymore, she pushed me forward. She believed in me, even when I was no one."

Lola had a sinking feeling. It didn't matter what his life was before—for Beau, money defined people. He actually believed he was nobody before it. "Where's your mom now?"

"With her sister in Florida. We aren't very close, but I support her how I can."

"With money," Lola said.

Beau pulsed his eyebrows once. "Not that she deserves it, but she's my mother after all."

"That's why you said money complicates things."

"One of the reasons."

"I'm sorry," Lola said.

"Everyone has things in their past to be sorry for. We can't let it shape who we are. Right?"

She glanced at her hands on the leather seat. She supposed everyone had things to be sorry for, but she'd made peace with her past. If that were true, there wasn't any reason why she shouldn't be honest with Beau about the fact that she used to strip. But was there any point in telling him now and risking that he'd see her differently?

"So," she said, "where are we headed next?"

"Let Warner worry about that. Tell me something, Lola. What've you got to be sorry for?"

"Not much," she said. "I'm not exactly a model citizen, but I have no regrets. My past *does* shape me. It's made me who I am. I don't believe in hiding from it."

"You've hidden things."

"Hidden? No. Not volunteered…yes."

"Why?" he asked. "Are you ashamed?"

As one of the few people she knew who'd actually learned from her past instead of buried it, she was almost offended. "You haven't earned the right to ask me that," she said.

"I'll earn it then."

He didn't have to. She was his for the rest of the night, and he could make all the demands he wanted.

"You might take it," she said, "but you won't earn it."

"I will. Trust me."

The way his voice had dropped when he'd said *trust me* made her want to do the opposite. It was becoming clear Beau had a weakness for a challenge. He'd showed her that at the L.A. Philharmonic gala, when he'd acted proud of being a bad chess player in high school because it meant an opportunity to improve. He'd said he was happiest when conquering himself, but she'd suspected he'd meant 'himself and others.'

"That kind of thing can't be earned in one night," she said. "And I promise, Beau—this is the last night we will ever spend together."

"Why? Your bank account's hit its limit?"

It was like being back at Hey Joe, when she'd been transfixed by Beau, and he'd nearly knocked her off her feet with his proposal. She curled her hands into two fists. "I don't get you. One minute you're tender and the next you've reduced me to nothing more than…than—"

"A whore?"

"Excuse me?" she asked, unable to keep the shock from her face. *He'd* put her in this position, and now he was accusing *her* of being a whore? "How dare you?"

"I'm being honest," he said. "A person who takes money in exchange for sex—what would you call her?"

Lola dug her fingernails into her palms with the urge to clock him.

"Maybe courtesan is better?" he asked. "It's more romantic."

Beau had a weakness for a challenge, but Lola's weakness, it turned out, was Beau. There was no other explanation for why she kept letting him in. He had a way of getting her to lower her shield so he could stick her with a knife. She didn't seem to learn her lesson. She leaned away from him. "Fuck you. I'm only doing all this because of you."

"You entered into this agreement willfully." He tried to take her hands, but she smacked him away and vaulted backward. He grabbed her wrists to pin her arms to her chest and her back against the seat. When she stopped resisting, he said, "I don't think you're a whore."

Her chest heaved. He was so close, she breathed on his face.

"But I'm going to fuck you like one tonight."

She wanted to fight back, protest, but she was melting at his touch, craving more of him despite his words. "You're awful. You treat me awful."

He kissed her. His grip never loosened, and she never stopped pushing back.

"Which one of us are you fighting, Lola?" he asked against her mouth. "Me or you?"

"I don't know," she moaned, trying to catch her breath. She was hot, and some of it was anger. She'd empathized with him. It meant a lot that he'd opened up to her. She hadn't been that vulnerable, even with Johnny, since he'd made her dance for him at Cat Shoppe. "You're doing it again."

"Doing what?"

"What you did to me last time."

"Can you be more specific?"

"First you make me comfortable. Loose. Then you try to humiliate me."

He released her and sat back. "I don't know what you're talking about."

"I'm right, aren't I? Last time you took me to a star-studded fundraiser so I'd be awed and see you at your best. Then suddenly you put me on stage and command me to strip. Tonight you take me to meet your sister, open up to me, then call me a whore?"

"My, my." The corner of his mouth crooked. "What an imagination you have." His smile vanished. "Remind me to punish you later for being so impertinent tonight."

"Nowhere in the terms did it say I couldn't fight back."

"But it did say I'd always win."

The threat in his tone resonated everywhere—in her heart, in her stomach, between her legs. Beau would always win, because whenever he decided tonight, he'd have her. As much as he wanted.

"Don't look so frightened, ma chatte." He took her chin in his hand and lifted her head. He trailed his fingers under her jaw and behind her neck. "I am going to love you in the way I fuck you. I'll make everything better," his voice dropped, "and worse."

He took his hand away, but his touch remained—a reminder that her body wasn't in her control. His words were just as unshakeable, and she quickly forgot about her body. Now she worried about his hold over the rest of her.

Chapter Eight

Lola hadn't noticed they were heading toward the Four Seasons until the limo turned into the hotel's half-moon drive. She looked at Beau. "Did you forget something?"

"No."

Her door opened. Fleetingly she'd wondered why she was even more dressed up than the week before while he was in a suit instead of a tuxedo. Now she had her answer—he just hadn't changed yet.

They unfolded from the car. Beau placed his hand at the center of her back. In the lobby, he guided her right, away from the elevators. "First, a drink."

He directed her to the hotel lounge. The few people seated around the room were as cool and modern as the bar's interior. They spoke and sipped their drinks privately. The bartender placed two napkins in front of them. "The usual, sir?"

"And the Colony Cocktail for her."

Beau had a "usual." Was it a girl and a Scotch, only his choice of drink the same night after night? What were the other girls like—and did they all have Colony Cocktails? Lola's dress was elegant—she was not. She wondered if anyone at the bar could tell, and moved closer to Beau.

He looked down and smoothed a hand over her hair. "All right?" he asked in her ear.

She was bothered thinking of him with another woman, but it hardly seemed fair to bring it up, not that she wanted to. It would only invite questions. She nodded that she was fine.

When their drinks were served, Beau picked a corner booth and they sank against the pillows. He clinked his Scotch against her glass. "To the night," he said. "Underneath its faithful cover, we can be who we want. Or in some cases, who we truly are."

"Or, *I* can be who *you* want," Lola said. She took a sip.

"Meaning?"

"This dress. The limo. The cocktail—too expensive, I might add. I'm simply a product of your fashioning."

"Or," he said, grinning, "a masterpiece sculpted from clay."

"Whatever you want to call it."

"I like to think the masterpiece is already there, underneath. I'm just chiseling the clay away."

"I was nothing until you came along. Is that what you mean?" In case her sarcasm was lost on him, she smirked. "Your money's made me worthy?"

96

He touched her knee. Her smirk faltered. "No. I like you just as you are. You don't pretend to be something you're not like most people I know." He slid his hand up her thigh, and it left a tingling sensation in its wake. She exhaled louder than she meant to. "You don't hide who you are, do you?" he asked.

Her focus was shifting from their conversation to his touch. She wasn't sure she grasped what he was getting at. "No."

"You wouldn't pretend with me."

She understood. Fighting their connection, keeping her feelings to herself—it was the same as hiding parts of herself from him. It went against who she claimed to be.

"It's not that black and white," she said. "Everyone has some darkness inside to hide what they need to." She paused. "Even you. Maybe you most of all."

He looked as surprised by her statement as she was. But it was true. She'd glimpsed his dark side here and there. It didn't scare her. The opposite, actually. It made her want to know more.

"Do you?" she asked.

"Like you said, everyone has some darkness."

"What's yours?" Even as the question came out, she knew he wouldn't answer. Beau seemed to have levels. He'd let her beneath the surface—somewhere she didn't think many people got—but then there were layers over his heart and his trust that not just anyone could peel away.

His hand on her thigh tightened. He glanced over at the bartender, absentmindedly watching him make a drink.

She regretted her question. It was her job to make sure her feelings stayed physical, but they were edging on dangerous territory. She *was* just anyone to him. She couldn't be the one to remove his layers. "Never mind," she said. "It's too much for just one night."

He quickly turned back to her. "No. It's okay. I'm just not used to talking about these things. That doesn't mean I don't…want to." He cleared his throat. "During the two years my mom was depressed, she stopped leaving the house and I took on all the responsibility. She'd say I was nothing like my dad. My dad would've run away, but I didn't. I took care of her. I spent time with her every day. I bought all the groceries and Brigitte and I would cook each night. I made sure the bills were paid and that Brigitte kept up with her schoolwork."

Lola had a familiar feeling in her gut. She'd also been forced to take care of herself, but at least she hadn't had other people depending on her too.

Beau rubbed the bridge of his nose. "It's just that none of that did anything. None of it was enough. The only thing that made her happy again was that money— Brigitte's inheritance. And once it was gone, she picked up and went to Florida." He looked up at her. "I couldn't take care of her—or anyone for that matter. My dad needed a whole other family, because I wasn't enough."

"I understand, Beau. My dad left too."

"I know." He studied her a moment. "Do you ever feel like you aren't enough?"

A lump formed in her throat. As a kid, it'd been straightforward, like an equation—if she could get her dad a bike, he'd come home. She thought she knew better now, but maybe she didn't. Beau didn't seem to. "Is that what drove you to work as hard as you did? Not being enough?"

"Is that why you're here tonight?" he countered.

They stared at each other. For once, Lola didn't try to shut him out. She held his gaze—let him strip her down for a few moments.

"You're afraid if Johnny loses Hey Joe, all he'll have left is you. You want to give him something else— his own bar, money, a family—because you think you alone aren't enough."

It sounded so simple when he put it that way, as if it hadn't been years building. It wasn't that she hadn't thought of the effect her dad leaving had on her relationship with Johnny, but when she did, it was in an abstract way. It wasn't the way Beau dealt with his insecurity, where money equaled love and there wasn't much more to it than that.

"And as long as you have money, you have something people want," she said. "Somebody can always be there if you need them. But it also means you don't have to let anyone get close."

"*You're* getting close."

"Why?" she asked. "Why are you telling me all this?"

JESSICA HAWKINS

He picked up his drink and swirled it. "I guess it's because I know nothing will continue past sunrise. It's almost like…"

"It doesn't count," she finished.

She and Beau weren't so different, but it wasn't just that they had something in common. Having the same fear over their heads and recognizing it in each other connected them deeper—in a way many people never did.

She covered his hand with hers. "You're enough without it." She swallowed. He winced. "Maybe the money is what got me here, but it was never what I wanted. It was a means to an end. I want you to know—in my eyes, you are enough without it."

He got closer, leaned into her. "Give me that too, Lola. Something no one else has. When I'm inside you tonight, when I take you, I want to know something about you he doesn't."

She shook her head.

He stroked some of her hair behind her ear. "I told you things I've never told anyone."

"Johnny knows everything," she whispered.

"There must be something. Close your eyes. Say it in the dark."

His clean, natural scent invaded. There was, in fact, something Johnny didn't know—something she didn't even want to admit to herself. Something that could only be said in the dark. She let her lids fall shut. "I'm here tonight because I want to be," Lola said. "Not because of the money or so I can buy him his dreams." She took a deep breath, fighting herself. Giving this to

100

Beau was like taking it from Johnny. "I'm here because every way you touched me last time was the right way and because it meant something to me."

"Lola," he murmured. He was so close that he swallowed her words before the world heard them. He kissed her softly. "*I* am exactly where I want to be—for the first time in a long while."

"I think you might be right that I didn't know what I wanted until you showed me."

His took her face in his hands firmly. "Yes. You need a man who can be that for you. A man worthy of your love."

"Love?" Her eyes flew open. "Wait—what?" She removed Beau's hands by his wrists with great effort. "That's not what I was saying. Love has nothing to do with any of this."

"It has everything to do with this. Is Johnny enough?" he asked. "Maybe I had it wrong before. Maybe you're more afraid *he* isn't enough, and without Hey Joe, it'll all fall apart."

Throughout their relationship, she'd catch herself feeling that way and snap out of it. The guilt of thinking he wasn't enough—when *her* fear was not being enough for him or anyone—could be suffocating. She'd buried it deeper any time it threatened to emerge. "He's enough," she said, but her voice was shaky. Unconvincing even to her own ears.

"I don't believe you. You need more. You deserve more. Did he do everything in his power to stop you from coming here tonight?"

"No, but—"

"Did he throw himself at your feet and beg you not to go through with it? Did he tell you if you did, you'd never see him again because he couldn't live with himself? Did he say he didn't care about the money—that without you, it would mean nothing?" He put one hand on the table, trapping her in the corner. "I would buy you over and over again, Lola, but I would never sell you. Not to see every dollar bill in the world stacked at my feet."

Lola's eyes darted between his. It couldn't be true. Beau hadn't known her long enough to make a declaration like that. But for some reason, she believed him. "Beau, I…I don't—"

"You should know what you're worth." He ran his hand through his hair. "It's his job to make sure you know."

She just shook her head. "I don't know how you expect me to respond to that."

"I don't." He smoothed the hair he'd just disturbed. "I'm not asking you for anything. I'm not saying I deserve you either. But be here with me tonight—just me. You might be surprised to learn that love comes in different packages, even ones tied in a black ribbon."

He stood and left the table.

Love? Was that what he wanted? Was he her doomed gift that should remain wrapped? Or was she the one topped with a black ribbon, left out to tempt him?

She found him waiting for the elevator and went to stand silently next to him.

He gathered her hair in his hand and let it fall down her back. "I got carried away," he said. "I think about all the late nights, all the things I missed out on for work. Fueled by just the smallest hope that one day I might have it all."

She looked up at his profile. He stared somewhere above the elevator. He seemed to have relaxed, but the hard angles of his jaw naturally made him appear tense.

"My youth. Family. Happy hour with co-workers. Women. Why did I do it? So I'd never want anything I couldn't have. So my family wouldn't want for anything, and so I could give another person everything she wanted when that time came. She'd have no reason to ever walk away from me." He glanced down at her. The elevator dinged. "That's what you're worth." He walked inside and turned to look at her. "Not a dollar amount. All those nights for these two nights with you."

"Me?" she asked. How was it she could have that much power over this man, who stood tall in his suit, looking capable of taking on the world in a moment's notice?

"Ironically," he said, "for a moment just now at that table, I thought I would give it all up for you. My kingdom for my queen."

Her footsteps echoed in the elevator bank as she followed him. She wrapped her arms around his middle. His body was stiff. She pressed her cheek against his chest. The elevator was like this moment between them, warm and private. The walls were wood paneled, except for the doors, which reflected their embrace as distorted and brassy. "If it weren't for him…if we'd met a different way. If things weren't how they are."

"You could love me?"

She wanted to give herself over completely, just for the space of one night, but she knew she wouldn't come out the other side the same. And at some point in her life, keeping things the same had become important to her. It was the threat of change that had gotten her to this place—that's how far she and Johnny had gone to keep things the same.

Could she love him? There were moments she and Beau were impossibly close for the short amount of time they'd spent together. He picked and picked at scabs that had formed over the wounds time had healed. She was most connected to him when he was also vulnerable, like just now in the lounge. When he took her there, they went together.

"Maybe. That's all I can give you." She couldn't risk her life with Johnny to love and be loved by Beau for one night. "Maybe I could love you."

"If at any hour of this night you think you do, tell me. Promise me that."

She should've laughed at the absurdity of it. Or come back with some witty response meant to deflect. But it wasn't funny. She'd lied to him. There was no "maybe." Her answer was yes—she could love him. Maybe part of her already did.

Chapter Nine

The presidential suite transported Lola to her first night with Beau when the air had been thick with sex and excess. Now the room seemed spotless. The door was already closed behind them. Lola looked to Beau, waiting.

He watched her too, his eyes suddenly and rudely penetrating as he loosened the knot of his tie. He slid it from around his neck and unbuttoned his collar. He moved behind her and lifted it over her head. "Have you been blindfolded before?" he asked, hovering it in front of her eyes.

"Once. Not seriously." At the beginning of their relationship, she and Johnny had spontaneously stopped in an adult toy store after a night out. They hadn't bought anything, but unexpected moments like that sometimes inspired Johnny to be more adventurous. That night, when they'd gotten home, they'd used one of her scarves. "It didn't last long after I hit my shin on the bedpost."

"Not with me. I won't let anything hurt you," Beau said as her world went black. The tie was cool and smooth on her lids, but rough where he knotted it against the back of her head. His hand slid up the nape of her neck. He grabbed her hair and kissed her under her ear. "Walk."

She took one step.

"Until I say stop."

She instinctively put her hands in front of her. He guided her by her hair until just her thighs were up against something smooth and cool, like wood. He never told her to stop. "What are we doing, Beau?" she asked. "Why are we here?"

He touched the skin on her lower back where her dress dipped. He slid his hands up to her exposed shoulder blades, under the beaded, crossed straps and yanked hard.

"Beau," she gasped when they snapped.

With another jerk, he split the dress down the back. Beads scattered, and the heavy dress slumped to the floor.

"What—"

"This was always the only destination," he said softly behind her.

He kissed her between the shoulder blades and guided the upper half of her body down with a firm hand. She folded into a mattress and realized she was bent over the footboard. "But the dress—"

"Is ruined." He separated her feet with the toe of his shoe and something silky brushed her bare calf. He dragged it up the inside of one thigh and slid it back and forth between her legs, rubbing it over her underwear. He wrapped it around her upper thigh.

"What are you doing?" she breathed.

"Don't force me to become a cliché by asking you to trust me."

She bit her lip when he pulled the fabric tight.

"I'm tying you to the bed," he said.

He moved to her other thigh.

"Are you comfortable?" he asked.

"Physically, yes. But I don't think I am with being tied down."

"That's fine." He ran his hand up the back of her leg and slapped the crease of her ass.

She winced. The sting resonated through her just as deliciously as it had the first night when he'd spanked her.

"Beautiful," he said. "I do appreciate the change in attitude where your undergarments are concerned."

She breathed from her mouth. "They aren't anything expensive, but—"

"They're perfect."

He pulled her thong down so it stretched over her thighs. She could picture it, the siren-red, lacy thing that molded to her hipbones, now bunched and cutting into her skin. Beau's fingers had barely grazed her legs.

Glass chimed against glass. The pungent smell of hard liquor hit her. "Beau…"

"Are you saying my name because you know what it does to me?"

Her unease at being blinded and bound had

dissolved as she'd anticipated his touch again, but it returned now. "I'm trying to trust you."

"But you want to know what I'm doing."

"Yes."

"I'm appreciating," he said with a resigned sigh. "If I were a less decent man, I'd take a picture right now to remember you by."

Lola's hands dashed to the blindfold. "You—"

"Don't take that off." His command came so strong, she froze. "I'm not going to take your picture. I told you to trust me. A camera wouldn't do you justice anyway."

She replaced her hands on the comforter. "You dress me up, bring me here, then make me spread my legs for your viewing pleasure while you have a Scotch?"

"Whiskey," he corrected.

"Scotch *is* whisky."

"Touché. Except this is the American sort."

"A technicality."

"Technicalities are not to be overlooked."

"Here's a technicality—you could not *be* a less decent man."

He laughed. "If you could see how beautiful you look right now, you'd understand how much I'm enjoying this."

"I doubt it."

He hummed. "Lose the attitude for a minute, Lola. Listen to what I see—possibly the most entrancing woman I've ever encountered, folded over my bed with her sweet pussy displayed. Just for me."

Her body thrilled with his words. Even

108

blindfolded, Lola had to shut her eyes. Her heels propped her ass in the air, and her black hair would be messy from Beau's tie. Without stockings, her legs would be long and white. Her body rose and fell faster on the mattress with each breath.

"The burn of quality alcohol in my throat," he continued, "while I think of what I want to do to you next. I didn't plan this part. If I'd let myself think of having you in this room again, I would've shown up at your front door and dragged you back here."

Beau's deep voice pushed its way into her. She gyrated her hips a little against the lip of the bed, trying to hit the right spot. He had that kind of control over her, even without touching her.

"I'm hard for you. I want to be inside you. But right now I need a moment to memorize the way your hands are clenching the sheets. Your red lips parting with each gasp. So fucking sue me. If this is my last night with you, I'm going to appreciate it."

She practically writhed on the mattress. "You're screwing with me, and it's working," she said. "I don't care. Am I supposed to admit I want you? I do. I'm ready."

His footsteps made little noise on the carpet, but she knew he was coming. There was a sudden, wet heaviness on her lower back. "Do not spill my drink," he said. "I'm taking off my belt."

She forced herself to keep from squirming.

"Now the rest of my clothes," he said. "My cock's reaching for you like you're food and it's been starving for months."

She turned her head so her other cheek pressed into the mattress. She was getting uncomfortably warm. She squeezed her eyes shut behind the blindfold.

He thumbed her cheeks apart, then her lips, opening her for him. Without her vision, she never knew where his fingers would probe her next, heightening her anticipation.

"You weren't lying about being ready." His crown collected her wetness, sliding up and down. "God, Lola. I must've sold my soul at some point for something this good."

Unable to take what she wanted, she was stunted but growing feisty. All she had were her words. "You think even the devil would have you?"

"He already does. He's got me."

"And you have me," Lola said. "You're my devil."

He thrust inside her all at once. She made a noise between a yelp and a moan as whiskey sloshed onto her back. Beau removed the glass and lapped up the liquid, his tongue slick and slippery, leaving goose bumps along her spine. "Whiskey and Lola," he said against her skin. "My new favorite flavor."

"You're going too slow," she said.

He dropped all of his weight on her back, sinking her body into the mattress. "How do you want me? Faster?" he whispered in her ear, picking up his pace. "Harder?"

"Yes," she said. "Yes to everything."

He slid his hand under her neck and lifted her head backward as he gave her what she wanted. "Waiting for you to come back was torture," he said while he fucked her. "Does that make you happy? Knowing how hard it's been for me?"

"No."

"Liar. You like to watch me suffer. Tell me I've owned you too."

He would never stop. He wanted more and more. She'd known this about him from the start—he was driven. Ambitious. Strong. She hadn't realized how it might be to have him go after her with all of that. She hadn't realized how much she'd want to give in. She bit her lip. "I'm the one who suffers."

"How?"

"I can't have what I want."

"What do—"

"You."

"I'm here, Lola. Right here."

She grit her teeth. Nothing mattered outside that moment. She could take what she wanted, and nobody would ever know but them. "You've owned me. Not just my body."

"How else?"

She was barely able to focus, but she still knew the things she could never say. *I could love you. If you don't stop, you'll own my heart too.* "I don't want to leave you," she said, her voice pitching.

"If I never untie you, you'll have no choice." He stopped moving. "Is that what you want? Me to take away your choice so you feel no guilt?"

"No," she said. "I don't know. Don't stop. Please."

"Tell me how you belong to me."

"I can't. You know what's true. Don't make me say

it."

With one hard thrust, he was pounding into her again. "Then tell me what's mine."

"My pussy is yours."

"*Bon petit chatte*," he groaned. "Keep talking."

"I don't want to say goodbye. I don't want to leave."

He pulled on her hair as she buried her head in the bed. The comforter muted her cries when her orgasm broke her apart from the inside, leaving her a shivering mess beneath him.

He didn't slow his rhythm. He took what he needed, hard, unrelenting, still pulling her hair, sucking on her earlobe, whispering almost inaudibly in her ear until he came too.

He didn't move off her for some time. Her breaths were soft whimpers. He removed the blindfold, but Lola's eyes were closed anyway. She sighed, only lifting her head when Beau pulled out. The white bedspread was smeared red from her lipstick.

Chapter Ten

Lola lay comfortably on her stomach while Beau propped himself up on one elbow next to her. He caressed her everywhere, from the marks on her thighs the ties had left behind up to her neck and shoulders.

She focused on Beau's touch on her skin to avoid feeling him anywhere else. It was as if he was inside her now—for good. He'd been fighting his way in, prying her open with words and caresses. She had no defenses when his only goal was her submission.

"You feel good," she whispered.

"You keep saying that. I'm afraid I'll get used to it."

She smiled and turned her head on the bed so she faced him. They looked at each other a moment. "About what I said—"

"Don't."

She closed her eyes. "Obviously I can't stay. I didn't mean it."

He cleared the hair from her face and then resumed stroking her back. "I know. Just don't leave me yet."

She shook her head. "I'm here. But if you don't keep talking, I might fall asleep."

"What do you want to talk about?"

"Anything. Whatever's on your mind."

"All right. Do you worry about getting pregnant?"

She made a startled noise. "Do you worry about killing the mood? Jesus. *That's* what's on your mind?"

"I'm curious," he said with a deep chuckle. "You don't seem worried."

"We already discussed birth control."

"It isn't a hundred percent effective."

She sighed. "I'd be worried if I thought of it, but I can't. I just can't. So I don't. It would be devastating."

"Would it?"

"To have the child of a man who bought me for a night? Yes."

"Funny how much tighter the knots in your back just got."

She couldn't even picture Beau as a dad—terse, uptight, suit-wearing Beau, picking up his toddler daughter on his way out the door to work as Lola watched, her hip against the counter, coffee in one hand, clutching her robe closed with the other. All of them smiling.

Or maybe she could.

She chewed the inside of her cheek. "Do you make all your partners sign a pregnancy waiver?"

"No, and it's not called a 'pregnancy waiver.'"

"You should be careful who you sleep with, you know. A lot of women would see an opportunity there and take advantage."

"I think you think I sleep around more than I do. And I use condoms always. It's not like those encounters are..."

"Prearranged?"

"Precisely."

There was certainly more to think about when you had money. Lola figured she might have to start looking over her shoulder as well. "Do you trust me?" she asked.

"I do, but I have to protect myself."

"Do you really trust me, or are you just saying that?"

He kneaded her shoulder hard. "That's a big one," he said after a few seconds.

"Happens when you work on your feet."

He kept working the knot. "Have you ever considered doing anything else?"

She didn't mind the topic change. He didn't have any reason to trust her, but she didn't want to know how it'd feel to hear him say it. "Once I applied as an office manager for a place in Century City."

"Did you get the job?" he asked.

"Yes. I turned it down. I couldn't bring myself to wear a suit to work."

"It's hard to pretend to be something else day after day."

"Most people just become what they're pretending to be."

"I suppose," he said. "Is it still your dream to become an office manager or did the wardrobe kill it for you?"

Her laugh sounded as contented as she was. "I told you, I don't dream. I didn't grow up with choices. Just options. Waitress. Cashier. That kind of thing."

"Says who?"

"It's just the truth about the life Johnny and I lead. Neither of us went to school or had opportunities. Johnny's parents get by, but not enough to help us out."

"You're a smart girl. Seems like you could've figured it out if you wanted."

"I guess it's possible that," she hesitated, "I got a little too comfortable at Hey Joe. But things will be different now."

"How?"

"I'll be on the business end of things. Making decisions, coming up with ideas."

"You won't continue bartending?" he asked in a way that sounded as if he already knew the answer.

"Well, I will in the beginning." She inhaled when he hit a sore spot in her lower back. "I'll keep doing that until things are running smoothly. Hopefully not more than a few years."

"Do you think things will change because of the money?" he asked.

"What do you mean?"

"If I were Johnny, things wouldn't be fine for me. I couldn't live with myself after this. Then again, I wouldn't have allowed it in the first place."

"You keep saying that," Lola said, "but you don't know. You made it nearly impossible for us to turn it down."

"That's true. I wouldn't have offered it if I hadn't known you'd accept."

"There's no way you could've known," she said. "I almost said no."

He was quiet a moment. "But you didn't."

No, she hadn't. And apparently he'd known all along what her answer would be. She pursed her lips. "You have issues, Beau. Anyone ever told you that?"

"Maybe an ex-girlfriend here or there."

If she could've rolled her eyes without opening them, she would have. "Is that why you don't have a girlfriend? Nobody can handle you?"

"No." He sounded offended, like a small boy. It made Lola smile, picturing him that way. "It's because nobody interests me at the moment."

"Not even me?" There was definite flirtatiousness in her question, but it was natural to be flirting in bed with the man who'd just done what he had to her.

"People or things that defy my expectations get my attention," Beau said. "So, to answer your question, yes, you do."

"Oh, I see. I get it," she said. "The trashy girl from the slums who doesn't put up with your shit. The one who tells you 'no' when you're constantly surrounded by yes men."

He grunted. "You've been watching too many movies."

"It's the truth, isn't it?"

"I'd be lying if I said I wasn't attracted to that side of you, but it isn't all you are, is it? You really should stop referring to yourself as trash."

"I was being facetious."

"But you believe it, even if you pretend not to be bothered by it."

She grew up in a poor neighborhood without a father. She'd been a teenage stripper. Lola had no disillusions about what people probably thought of her. If that was their conclusion, better that she beat them to it. That didn't mean she believed it. "Admit it. You must've thought that, even a little, when you first met me."

"I didn't. And I don't want to hear it again. It's beginning to irk me."

"Well," she said, sighing, "I wouldn't want to irk you."

"Not sure I believe that."

He continued to rub her back, occasionally massaging her shoulders or ass. "Are you sleeping?" he asked after a while.

"Yes."

"So you never pretended to be a singer or a teacher or President like other kids?"

"We're still discussing this?"

"I'm just trying to understand you better."

"I didn't play like that," she said. "I had my one Barbie, and we were just fine."

"What a shame."

She agreed—it was a shame. She didn't remember where she'd even gotten a Barbie. Her mom hadn't been much for typically girly things like dolls or Disney princess movies. Lola blinked out of her haze a little as the memory came to her. "Wait. Actually, she wasn't even a real Barbie. She was a knock-off Barbie I found at a daycare and named Nadia after the babysitter. My neighbor made her have simulated sex with her authentic Ken doll, and then she threw Nadia on the ground after."

"That's," Beau blew out a short laugh, "the most depressing thing I've ever heard."

"Then I'll stop there."

"Why, what happened next? Skipper kicked her into the street and she was run over by a semi?"

"Probably something like that." She couldn't help laughing but then got quiet. She was awake again, Beau touching her, make her warm. What time was it? How long had they been talking? "Why are we talking about this? Really, you're not very good at paying for sex."

"For what it's worth, Nadia sounds like a hell of a lot more fun than Barbie."

"She can certainly take more."

"I like a woman who doesn't break when you bend her."

"Nadia wouldn't," Lola said.

"What really happened to her?"

"No idea," Lola said. "One day I went to look for her, and she was just gone."

"I'm sorry to hear that."

"Just as well. I was looking for her to throw her out."

"Why?" he asked.

"Someone at school said dolls were for babies. I hadn't played with her in years, but I still wanted to get rid of her. I didn't want anyone thinking I was a baby."

"I can't imagine anyone accusing you of that."

"They didn't. I may not have had much growing up, but I had the respect of my peers." Respect had never been a problem for her, no matter her age, even with those who'd known how she was making her money. "If only they could see me now."

Beau kissed her hair above her ear. "Don't be so hard on yourself."

"Right. That's your job."

"A job any other man would envy."

She pressed her lips together, smiling a little. "What about you, Beau? Do you have any regrets about what do you for a living?"

"None."

"Why? What specifically about it makes you happy?"

"It's the perfect setup. I use my money to make more money. That's something I can see and understand. Of course, there are no guarantees when it comes to these things, but we're very thorough in our research and projections. Generally the companies we choose are poised for success. So far, thanks to that and a little luck, the returns have been incomparable."

"Not buying it," Lola said immediately. "What is it that drives you every day? What makes you smile?"

Beau was silent as if deciding how to respond. Finally, he said, "I guess it would be giving someone a chance at his dream. Not many people in this world have that gift to give. Some of these people are kids still—twenty-two, twenty-three—they work so fucking hard just on the belief they have what it takes. Like I did."

"You like helping them," she said. "You give them more than just money."

"Before I make any decisions, I have to get to know the founders. Really know them, their values and how they do business. That's why I brought those two guys to your bar with me. If I'd taken them to an expensive restaurant, they would've clammed right up. They needed a place like Hey Joe, where they were comfortable and could be themselves so I could see what I was investing in."

"You do that with all your potential ventures?" It was clear to Lola she wasn't just a deal Beau had made, but an actual person he took interest in. Beau had led those guys down a path of his design in order to understand them. The way he'd mapped out his dates with Lola. Did that make her like them, though? If so, she wasn't much of an investment at all. She produced no returns.

"I do," he said. "Intuition is a driving factor in many of my decisions."

"So if Mayor Churchill meets with you one on one, he'll understand your intentions. And then tax breaks for you and your friends means more investment money and more opportunities to give."

He laughed. "I don't know about calling all the rich people in Los Angeles my friends, but otherwise yes.

And that's just the start. I'd love to get more incentives for startups here so they'll consider L.A."

"What else?" Lola asked. Ideas excited her. Acting on them. It was what Hey Joe needed to turn around. Passion, ambition, motivation. Someone to take the lead and bump them past the level of talking about what they should do next. For a fleeting, shameful moment, feeding off Beau's enthusiasm, Lola wished Johnny were more like Beau in that sense.

"Coding needs to be mandatory in high schools," Beau said, "but offered as early as elementary level. If I'd taken it in school, I'd be light years ahead of where I am, and I'm already pretty advanced. Girls need to be educated that technology's not just for boys. I put on this yearly conference free for aspiring or existing entrepreneurs, and there are a few sessions for those under eighteen who're interested."

"Back up. A conference for entrepreneurs?" she asked. "You put it on?"

"My company, Bolt Ventures, does. But it's really a personal project for me. It's one weekend in Los Angeles with workshops, panels, free legal advice, things like that. And entrepreneurs with a business plan get to pitch their ideas to investors with five-minute, rapid-fire presentations. There's also opportunities for one-on-one time with people who've been in their shoes and succeeded."

"Wow," Lola said. "I admit—I'm a little shocked. What do you get out of it?"

"Nothing, really."

"That can't be. Exposure maybe?"

"I got screwed over with my first company, and I didn't even realize it at first."

"Didn't you make millions off that deal?"

"Yes, but once they had my company, they didn't value the work I'd put into it. I guess this conference is a way of providing the tools I didn't have so others don't have to make decisions they shouldn't be making without all the information."

Lola struggled to envision a world where a ravenous, bulldozing businessman like Beau Olivier did something so selfless.

"There's some exposure for Bolt. People in the industry know I'm behind it. They have to. I need my contacts to make it successful. But it's maybe the one business venture I do that's not for financial gain. It's for them."

"I don't think I've ever heard you this passionate," Lola said, her eyes still shut.

Beau snorted. "Do I have to tell you you're wrong about that?"

Her cheeks warmed. "You might be right."

He moved hair off her face. "You must've been a cute little Lola."

"That's what you got from the picture I painted earlier?"

"No. I got that from the way you just scrunched up your nose when you smiled." He fell quiet again, raking his fingers through her hair. "I want to know what that girl thought her future looked like. Maybe it's something I could give you."

He'd already afforded her one future. With two million dollars, she and Johnny could do anything. She parted her lips to ask him what more he could possibly give her, but she closed her mouth. It was a question that could lead them down many dangerous paths—what could he offer her that she didn't already have with Johnny?

She opened her eyes, blinking several times to adjust to the light. In the dark, it'd almost been as if she'd dreamed the past few hours. "We're just supposed to be having sex," she said. "All these questions about my past—my future? I hope you aren't falling in love with me."

"I can't tell if you're joking. But what if I were?"

Her heart pulsed, even though she knew that was impossible—impossible for anyone, but even more so for people like them, who'd had to grow an extra layer around their hearts. "You can't fall in love with someone in a night."

"Just like you can't buy a person?"

"What?"

"Nothing. Never mind."

Lola stared at his naked pecs. Whenever he worked out a kink in her back, there was obvious strength in his hands. Now she watched the muscles in his arm and chest tighten.

She'd told Johnny she loved him on a weekday. It wasn't anything worth remembering, like during an expensive dinner or an especially gripping orgasm. She'd just worked a shift at Cat Shoppe, and it'd been late. Her body had dragged like it was made of lead. He'd been in the parking lot, waiting to give her a ride. She'd been so grateful for not having to take the bus home that it just came out. She'd had no idea back then whether she really loved him, only that it felt right to say it.

"It's not possible," Lola murmured out loud. "Not in one night."

Beau bent to peck her cheek. She tilted her head up and met him with her mouth. He pulled her closer by her nape. Their tongues were slow, gradual, tasting. Probing. Then consuming.

Lola thrummed, partly from listening to Beau talk about his work. It added a dimension to him she hadn't known much about. His drive was sexy, the way he commanded all of her in the bedroom was.

Just as she was about to climb on top of him, he pulled away and put a hand on her back to keep her on her stomach. The mattress sank as he straddled her. He grabbed lotion she hadn't noticed before from the bedside table. Next to it was a bottle of lube. He squeezed the lotion onto her back and tossed the bottle aside. His hands became even more powerful over her skin.

She tried to tell him how good it was, but she could barely make noise. He kneaded his fingers up her neck, into her hair, then down to her shoulders, her lower back. He dipped them between her legs. He squeezed and separated her ass cheeks, letting his thumbs run along the insides.

"Beau," she murmured. With a shock of cold on her lower back, she opened her eyes. The lube was also gone from the nightstand.

"Relax," he said. He dropped his hand lower, spread the lube around and added more.

"I can't," she said.

His throat sounded raw. "Can't what?"

She bit her lip when he circled around her clit. "I know where you're going with this." She swallowed and exhaled against the bed. He took his hand away. He hovered over her back as he kissed his way from one shoulder blade to the other. Her attention struggled between following his lips and the insistent hardness against her thigh.

"The way you melt into the mattress like this," he said quietly, brushing his mouth down her spine to the center of her back, "it gets me insane. Turns me on like crazy."

His hand returned between her lubed cheeks, and he pressed a finger against the one place it couldn't be. Her reflex was to blush furiously. She considered herself adventurous in the bedroom except when it came to this. She hadn't let Johnny anywhere near her ass until years after they'd started dating. Everything in her body coiled into a tight spring with a mixture of fear and anticipation.

"Don't brace yourself." His other hand rubbed her lower back firmly, coaxing her. When he was demanding, she was powerless to him—when he was gentle, like he was now, she lost all control over herself.

He worked a finger inside her, and her awareness of anything other than its snug fit vanished. He slid it out slowly then back in, massaging her at an easy, relaxed pace. Her embarrassment waned, but her face burned hotter with a mix of emotions. She liked what he was doing, but she worried anything more would hurt.

She'd only let Johnny get as far as this, but he hadn't been as calm as Beau about it. She hadn't enjoyed it. It was almost as if Beau were touching a different spot than Johnny had. Beau did this for her, not for himself. She was no longer bracing herself.

"Good," he said, grit in his voice. "You're doing good."

Pride swelled in her. She wanted to prove to him she could enjoy it, elicit more praise. As he added a second finger, she focused on her breathing through the initial bite of pain. Soon, as his probing became deeper, quicker, she not only accepted him inside her but wanted him there.

"God," she exhaled, "damn."

His only response was a low grunt and to stretch her even more with another finger. She'd warmed to him and deep in her belly, gradually, a knot of pleasure began to form. She curled her hands in and out of balls around the comforter. He withdrew his fingers without warning and in their place came a much heavier pressure.

"Wait," she said.

He rubbed the head of his dick against her puckered opening. "I'll stay gentle," Beau said, coating them both in more lube. Though the pain worried her, it wasn't enough to stop her. She was too turned on to tell him no for that reason alone. It was that this was something she'd never given Johnny—something he wouldn't forgive if he found out.

"I can't let you have this," she said.

He slid the length of his shaft between her cheeks. "Why not?"

"I've never…" Sharing her and Johnny's sex life with Beau seemed wrong. Everything was wrong—him pressing against such an intimate place, her not only allowing it, but wanting it, when she never had before. But those things were also spurring on her arousal. "I just can't…shouldn't."

"It's part of the deal." He sounded frayed, edgy with impatience as one of his hands kneaded her ass cheek. "When and how I want." He blew out an exhale. "Where."

"Johnny's tried, and I've told him no every time. He's begged me, Beau. You don't understand what this means."

He put one elbow by her head and closed his body over her back. "Yes, I do," he said into her hair, "and it only makes me want it more." The tip of his cock intruded on her, begging to enter. "Remember how good it felt to submit to me?" His hot breath warmed her ear. "That's all this is. Yielding. Taking everything I give you, because that is our arrangement. Because you like it that way."

She'd been determined not to let Beau have this. He had the power to turn her body against her, though—her mind too. He would never be satisfied. This was her last defense against him, but he'd reduced her to a quivering mess and set her on a fragile, tenuous edge that might give any moment and plunge her into absolute vulnerability.

"I want this part as mine." His insistent pressing gave way to short, slick strokes as he entered her. It stung and throbbed, and her instinct was to reject the invasion, to recoil, to push him out, but whenever she tensed, he released a *shh* into her hair then kissed her in the same spot, waiting until she calmed. Her blood seemed to simultaneously rush and drain through and from her body. He was *big*, unfairly *big* it seemed in that moment, so much that she almost wished Johnny, not quite as *big*, had broken her in first.

"You're so tight. Let me fuck your ass, Lola, your tight virgin ass—not because I want it. Do it because you want me to have it."

He inched in. Didn't he know he could have whatever he wanted? Not because they'd agreed to it, but because she was utterly *consumed* with him, irrevocably *owned* by him? The pain was nothing to give him this—one more thing to link them together long after they'd said goodbye. He'd always be the first to feel her this way, to break down her every last barrier.

He pulled out and edged in deeper. She felt a little more of him and hurt a little less with each push. "That's it," he said. "Just relax. Let me do all the work."

She swallowed and swallowed, her throat impossibly dry. He moved off her body, and she realized she was sweating—or he was, or they both were. He put both hands on her ass and leaned into her, spreading her, thrusting, splitting her apart, holding her together. All she could do was groan, unable to process so much happening at once.

"All right?" he asked. He was gritting his teeth.

Every part of her that touched the bed was sweating now. "Yes," she exhaled.

"I won't last long. Just watching you is enough." When she'd think he was all the way in, he'd pull out a little and go deeper still. "Give me your hand," he said.

She bent her arm around to her lower back, and he laced his fingers with hers. He picked up speed, became less gentle. She couldn't tell who was grasping whose hand.

Any shame she'd been clinging to dissolved as he fucked her most intimate spot. He filled her, all of her, discovering her, claiming her—from the inside. She had to know he was feeling this too. "What's it like for you?" she asked.

"I just feel you, baby, like fucking heaven." He panted over her, squeezing the life out of her ass and her hand. He stopped moving, still squeezing, still panting. "I want you to feel me back," he said. "Move on me. Make yourself come."

She was hesitant at first, even though she would've done anything he asked at that moment. It was counterintuitive, but she pushed back onto him, then forward into the mattress. She did it again—back and forth, her hips up and down, riding him slowly, taking every inch. When her need surpassed her timidity, she gyrated harder, faster, grinding against the bed, feeling his cock so fat inside her that there wasn't room for anything else in her body. She became fueled by an insane need to get off, by Beau's primal grunts she'd never heard before—not even the times he'd fucked her to the hilt, every muscle in his body strained. Her backing onto him was doing something to them both. Her fist was a vise around the comforter as she pulled and pushed. She opened her mouth, but her screams were silent, that was how hard she came—so intense and blinding, so unlike anything she'd felt before.

"I'm going to come already," he said, cutting right through her haze. "I can't watch you come apart like that. I need to go fast. Relax everything except your grip around my hand."

She held him tightly, biting her lip as he pulled out of her slowly. She was immediately empty without him.

He took her arm. "Come. Up. Hurry."

He couldn't get her off the bed and into the bathroom fast enough. He ran one hand over his cock as he flipped on the shower and tested the water with his hand.

"In," he commanded.

She got under the water before him. He hugged her from behind, grasping her breasts and sucking a spot under her ear. Her hair slickened. He was insistently hard against her backside. "Thank you," he murmured. "Thank you, Lola."

She fumbled with the hotel soap and threw the plastic wrapper on the ground. After lathering it, she turned around and took him in her hand.

"Ah," he gasped up at the ceiling. "Lola."

She cleaned him, rubbed him, worked him with two hands and still couldn't feel all of him at once. When she looked up, he was also watching. Water dripped from his hair, down his nose.

"You're sexy," she whispered.

His eyes jumped to hers.

"I don't think I ever told you because I'm supposed to hate you," she said, "but you're so handsome it hurts. And so sexy."

His Adam's apple bobbed when he swallowed. "You—"

"No," she said. "This is about you."

She climbed his cock with both her hands, one after the other, faster and faster. He made an expression she'd never seen on a person, something almost pained. But neither of them looked away. He leaned in, took her mouth with his and lifted her by her ass. He pressed her back up against the shower wall with the force of his kiss.

"*Ma lumiére*," he said hotly in her ear as he searched for her with his hand. He found her slick and teased her opening with his cock before entering her. "It means my light. So sweet, so soft, you are the light in my world tonight."

Her fingertips did everything but consume his textured jaw, his pliant hair, his wide, hard back and tensed shoulder blades. She was forced to stop touching to hang around his neck when his thrusts came too fast and out of control. The shower steamed over as hot water rained against his back and her limbs around him. She was warm everywhere except for her back, which slipped and slid over the cold marble.

"I'm going to come," he said, a hint of a growl in his voice. "Kiss me."

She drew back and let herself be devoured as he took her in every way. He thrust deep and came with his mouth on hers and his fingers denting her ass cheeks.

He removed one hand and ran it between them, gliding it over her wet skin and taking her breast in his hand. He released her to touch her clit.

"I can't, not again," she whimpered. She was raw, sore, used, but his deft fingers relentlessly rubbed her. She put her head back against the wall and gasped up at the ceiling.

He kissed along her neck and the underside of her jaw, running a course up to her ear and finding his way back to her mouth.

She could, and she did—she constricted her arms around him with all her strength as her orgasm roiled through her.

They breathed hard, he into her shoulder, she into his damp hair. Even when she became aware she was still clinging to him, she didn't loosen her grip. From start to finish, it had been too good to be true. She was afraid if she let go, he'd disappear.

"Lola," he whispered eventually. "Are you all right? Did I hurt you?"

She shook her head against his neck.

"Say something. Anything."

"I can't," she said. "I just gave you everything."

He stroked her hair with his hand, pressed his lips to the same spot, to her temple then her cheek until they were mouth to mouth again. He let the wall take her weight and kissed her like he did everything else—unforgiving, firm, but with attention to every detail.

She'd thought he couldn't possibly possess her any more after their first night, but each time he was inside her, they became even closer. Her chest stuttered, and her eyes welled. She didn't want to stop the kiss—she wouldn't let him see her cry. She was overwhelmed, and it clouded her mind. Whatever was making her feel this way wouldn't be fought off. Was it love? It wasn't the same thing she had with Johnny, so she couldn't be sure.

She pulled back anyway, needing to see his eyes.

"What is it?" he asked, blinking his wet lashes.

She hated to lose his green even for that second. "I don't know," she admitted. "How do you do it?" She ran her thumb over the corner of his eye. "Are you like this with everyone?"

"No," he said, all his severity in that one word.

"Why me?"

"Why you, Lola? When I see inside you, it always feels like the first time."

"You can see inside me?" she asked.

"Can't you feel me there?"

She knew she should look away. Immediately. When had they crossed into this territory? He was gaining traction where he never should've been in the first place. If she didn't stop him now, he'd only sink his claws in deeper. She had to give in or fight back. Beau wouldn't allow anything in between. She could no longer stand anything in between.

Her heart pounded as if magnetized to the thumping organ directly across from it. Her teeth fretted against her bottom lip.

Could she feel him there? Like a thunderstorm.

She pulled him back into the kiss and gave him anything she had left. She told him with her kiss what she couldn't with her words—Beau had her. Body, heart and soul.

Chapter Eleven

The city still stood, even though Lola's world had shifted. She was thankful for the bedroom balcony that gave her what she needed in that moment—fresh air. Fresh perspective. Whatever was in that room, it was getting to her.

How could she have let herself get so wrapped up in Beau? Johnny had said since she'd already done this once, a second time wouldn't be a big deal. How foolish they had been. This time was an even bigger deal—this time, Beau demanded more from her and she was hardly putting up a fight. Because she no longer had the desire to. What had she bitingly told Beau in the beginning?

"I'm sorry if you thought any amount of money would get you my heart."

She should've known if Beau decided that was what he wanted, that was what he'd get. The money no longer even registered for Lola—it was something else entirely. She and Johnny now had bigger problems.

Beau enfolded her from behind with his arms and rested his chin on her robed shoulder. "So you didn't run out on me," he said.

"I just needed a minute."

"I want to give you lots of things," he said, "but minutes aren't one of them."

"There's still half the night left." With her own words, she brightened. She and Johnny needed to have a conversation when she got home, but for now, she wanted to forget anything but being with Beau. "You should've taken me to dinner or something. What are we supposed to do until sunrise?"

"I don't know. I'm all fucked out for the moment."

She laughed and relaxed into his arms. "Me too."

"We could sleep," he suggested.

"Does that mean I have to give you a discount?"

He tsked in her ear. "Since when are we joking about this?"

She shrugged. "Since I've finally accepted this is how things are—this is our situation."

"Really. After all this, with only half a night left, you've finally accepted it?"

"Better late than never." It hit her then. There wasn't "still" half a night left—there was "only" half. Lola couldn't deny her feelings for Beau, but she and Johnny had history, and a lot of love between them. Aside from that, Beau hadn't signed on for anything more than a night. So after sunrise, she and Beau were finished. "You know something?"

"Tell me, beautiful."

138

"I don't think I want to sleep, because—" She hadn't thought through what she was about to say. It was a huge admission. She wavered, swallowing as if she could keep the words down.

Beau nuzzled into her hair. "Hmm?"

"Because this isn't just your last night with me," she said. "It's mine with you."

He kissed her cheek. "This is our space," he said softly. "You can always say what's on your mind, and nobody will know but us."

His arms were surrounding her. She was protected, but it was more than that. She was safe. While she was with him in their space, nothing could harm them. Nothing but themselves, she thought, right before pushing it out of her head.

"We can do whatever your heart desires with the time we have left," he said. "We can go to goddamn Paris if you want."

"I don't think our agreement holds across international lines."

"Yes, it does."

She shook her head. "I don't think so. There was no mention of that in anything I signed. I mean, for God's sake, what if I got pregnant in Paris?"

"Well—"

"That wasn't covered in the pregnancy waiver," she continued. "How would we proceed? And then there's the fact that we'd never make it back in time for sunrise—unless," she put a finger to her lips, "we adjusted for time change—"

He nipped the shell of her ear. "You're teasing me."

She giggled and covered his arms at her middle. "You're the only one who gets to have fun?"

"You're having fun. I know you are."

"You seem determined that I do. Why?" she asked, looking up at the sky. "Why do I matter to you?"

"Why does anyone matter to anyone? You're asking me to explain something impossible."

It still bothered her, though, that he'd never given her a reason. To pay that much just because he was drawn to her? Was that enough? She sighed. "Try."

"If you think any of this would be happening if you weren't you, you'd be wrong. It's not that I paid for a night with a woman. It's not that you're so beautiful, it almost hurts me."

The same was tragically true for Lola. She was there because of Beau, and she suspected that'd been the case all along. Johnny's happiness and Hey Joe's preservation were the reasons she'd convinced herself she could do it. She would've denied it until her last breath, but now she knew without a doubt—she would've refused anyone else's offer.

"What was the reason then?" she asked.

"That I simply had to have *you*. Can't you understand that? And maybe, can't you admit you understand because you feel the same for me?"

She was quiet. To know that herself was scary enough, but to say it out loud was traitorous—and it was terrifying. It could set something in motion, and she wasn't ready for that. There was nothing to be gained by a confession like that except more damage.

"Don't feel guilty, Lola. Johnny knew this was a possibility. There's no rule we can't fall for each other."

She looked over the balcony railing. "Maybe not. But I can't jump, Beau."

"There's more than one way to fall," he said. "Say, if you were pushed."

"If you push me," she said to the ground sixteen floors below, "it will be messy."

"It already is messy," he said. "Just trust in this— my hands on you."

His protection. A safe place in his arms. Nothing about him was trustworthy. Anyone who made as much money as him had to have put his needs ahead of everyone else's at some point. And he used that money to get anything he wanted, including her. When he was interested in a company, he designed their meetings around what made them most comfortable. Was that because he cared, or was it manipulation?

A thought struck her for the first time. Had his proposition at Hey Joe been spur of the moment like she'd thought, or had he done it there because that was where *she* was most comfortable?

"When was the first time?" she asked.

"The first time for what?"

"You said in the shower when you look inside me, it's always like the first time. When? What moment?"

He was silent for so long, she began to worry.

"Beau?"

"It was at the beginning," he said.

"The beginning of what? At Hey Joe? Or you mean the first night we spent together?"

"No," he said. He squeezed her so hard that she gasped a little.

"Beau?" she asked again.

"Remember at Hey Joe, before I left, I tried to tip you."

"Yes, I remember." Of all the moments and silences they'd had between them, that one was fairly insignificant in Lola's mind. "It was then?"

"No," he said. "Why didn't you take it?"

She mostly remembered it because it was right before he'd shifted from a mysterious, attractive man to a man who'd thought she could be bought. A lifetime had happened since then. "We'd been flirting," she said. "You asked me if I was attracted to you, and I was, but I couldn't say it. When you tried to give me that much money, it seemed somehow connected to that. Like you were cheapening our time together."

"I wasn't. I genuinely meant it to be nice."

"'Nice' isn't giving people money. It's giving them things money can't buy, like how you took me to that speakeasy because you thought I'd like it. Or letting me get syrup on your bed because it made me happy." She paused. "I don't care about your money."

His entire body tensed around her.

"But I know you worked hard for it. That's what I—" She caught herself before she could say it was what she loved about him. "It's what I care about. Your passion and drive, and that you love to help people create."

"You're reading too much into what I do."

"No, I'm not. I see you, Beau." She saw him, but she couldn't have him. Not when she and Johnny had given each other nine years of their lives, and not when she owed him more. "Why'd you ask about the tip?"

He shook his head on her shoulder. "Never mind."

"Beau—"

"Stop looking over the balcony. You're making me nervous." There was an edge to his voice, even though he held her tightly enough that she wasn't going anywhere. He hadn't answered her question, but she didn't want to spend what little time they had left arguing.

She blinked her eyes to the sky again. "All right. Is up okay?"

"Up is okay."

"You asked what I wanted to do tonight," she said. "I'd like to see the stars with you."

Beau's chin remained on her shoulder, and *he* was still looking over the balcony. "Can't see them now?"

"Not enough of them. I want to see them all."

He kissed the side of her head over her hair. "Go get dressed."

"Really?"

"I can do spontaneous. I know a place. I have to make a call, but I'll only be a moment."

"In the middle of the night?"

"Business overseas."

"Oh." She nodded. "Wait, what about—"

"In the closet," he said. "I have some things in there you can wear."

143

Things she could wear? Her jaw set. "If you think I'm wearing another woman's clothes—"

"They've never been worn," he said. "They're yours. I can be spontaneous—rarely—but I am also always prepared if I can help it."

That certainly sounded like him. She extricated herself from his grasp, went inside and found a couple plain, jersey women's T-shirts hanging in the closet. She chose one the muted color of raw clay. The jeans were almost equally as soft, and on the floor sat a pair of brilliant-white Chucks in her size.

She was dressed and combing her damp hair when Beau came into the bathroom. He also wore a T-shirt and jeans.

"We almost look like a normal couple," Lola said to his reflection in the mirror.

He frowned, watching her.

"Is everything okay?"

"Fine," he said. "Everything's fine. You ready?"

The look on his face matched his cross voice on the balcony. She'd seen him that way before—and since it was on her mind, she realized one of those times was right after she'd refused his tip. Before she could think anything of it, his face relaxed with a smile.

"Yes," she said. "I'm ready."

Downstairs, the valet ran for Beau's car, seeming eager for something to do in the middle of the night.

Beau took her hand as if it were the most natural thing. "I've been riding without the top lately," he said when the valet pulled the car up. "You've liberated me."

She smiled. "That's a nice thing to do to someone."

The roads were relatively quiet at that hour, and Beau took advantage of it. He turned up the music. The drive was all at once fast and slow, the speedometer needle climbing to sixty, seventy, eighty before Beau would let up on the gas. The wind had a way of soothing her conscience and wiping her clean, as if she were moving into a new state of awareness. She could no longer hide the truth about her feelings for Beau from herself. It was past midnight—the end of one day, the start of another.

They climbed the Santa Monica Mountains. Beau hugged each curve and took the sharp ones without flinching, anticipating them like he'd laid the pavement himself.

Neither of them spoke, but once in a while, Beau would look over at her and she couldn't help looking back. Then he'd return his eyes to the precarious, winding road, and she'd allow herself a few more seconds of Beau's hair, disheveled by the wind, and the stubble that had tickled her earlier. She hoped she'd get to feel the same burn as their first night together when he hadn't shaved—how long would it take for it to grow a little longer? Did they have that much time? To feel that kind of thing over her lips, along her jaw, between her legs—it was ownership.

Beau eventually slowed the car to a stop, pulling over to a lookout point.

"Mulholland Drive?" she asked. "I thought you knew a place."

"I do. This is it."

"Every Angeleno worth his salt knows about Mulholland."

He laughed loudly and looked up past the open roof. "So much for trying to impress you."

"If you're trying to impress me, you're going to have to do better than a stunning view and some orgasms."

He made a noise and raised an eyebrow at her. "Careful or you'll wake the beast again."

"By saying 'orgasm'?"

"He's easily aroused."

She rolled her eyes.

"I saw that," he said.

"How?" she exclaimed. "It's nighttime."

"Not all of night is dark. There's the moon, the stars."

"Just like even dark people have light, right? Is that what you're getting at?"

"You think everything I say has another meaning."

She turned in her seat to face him. "I thought to make an offer like you did that you must be a monster. Now I don't know what to think."

"I appreciate your candor," he said dryly.

"I'm just trying to figure this out. Figure you out. How can someone be anything other than morally bankrupt and vile to pay another man's girlfriend for sex?"

He dropped his hands along the curves of the steering wheel. "You're looking at it from the wrong angle, Lola. I'm a man who doesn't let anything get in the way of what I want. If my bank account had a zero balance and I wanted you badly enough...I wouldn't let that stop me. I'd find a way to get you."

"You make it sound so simple—like people are commodities." She paused, waiting for a response. She supposed maybe he had thought of her that way once. "By your own logic, there's nothing you can't have."

"I like to believe that." He looked over at her. "Why?"

Deep inside her not hours ago, he'd said he wouldn't let her go. Lola had made her own heated promises—why? To get to the finish line? Or because they were true and nothing counted in those lust-fogged moments? Beau had said if he wanted something badly enough, he'd go after it. It knotted her stomach to think of a Johnny-Beau showdown in which she'd have to choose between them. "Never mind."

Beau glanced over his shoulder and back at her. "I've never been here at night, but I should've guessed it would be closed."

Just behind him was a lookout point with a view of downtown Los Angeles. Lola had been going there since she was a teenager, often at night. Sometimes to drink with her friends, which seemed reckless now.

"There are ways around the gate," she said.

He arched an eyebrow at her. "You want to sneak in?"

"Would you?"

"We drove all the way up here." He went to open his door, but Lola put her hand on his forearm. He turned back.

"I don't need it," she said. "I've seen it. Let's just sit together."

He settled back into his seat. "Describe it to me."

"The sky is black, but the lights glow. Orange, green, yellow." She wiggled her pointer finger in the air. "Little dots. The buildings are like music bars of light and dark." She glanced up. "More often than you'd think, you can catch a shooting star. But right now, everything is mostly…still."

"Sounds almost perfect. But we're missing something." He shifted in his seat to dig in his pocket. "Vodka and Cheez-Its."

She half smiled. "What?"

"From the minibar." He held up a tiny bottle between two fingers and a bag in his palm. "I also brought tequila—if you're feeling adventurous."

"A surprise picnic under the stars? You're really clueless when it comes to wooing women, aren't you?"

"Take that back or you get no tequila." He twisted off the cap, took a sip and quickly shook his head. His thick hair, relaxed for once because of their shower, took a moment to settle. He blew out a breath. "Jesus. Now I remember why I don't drink tequila straight anymore."

Lola grinned. "Suck it up, pretty boy."

"Pretty boy? I take offense to that."

"It was intended to offend."

He laughed and passed the bottle. She finished it off as Beau watched her.

"And that's how it's done," she declared right before turning her face away to cringe.

148

"Busted," he said.

"I was just clearing my throat."

"Seriously? I know what I saw."

"I'll prove it," she said. "Pass the vodka."

He surrendered it to her with one palm in the air. "Yes, ma'am."

She opened it, downed half of it easily and offered him the rest.

He shook his head. "No more while I'm driving precious cargo."

Her eyebrows furrowed. "Precious—?"

There was that laugh again, deeper this time from the bottom of his throat. She wanted to bottle that sound and save it for later. For when they'd parted ways. She had to push the thought away quickly to stay in their moment.

"God, you're cute," he said. "*You*, Lola. You're the precious cargo."

"Oh," she said, warm in the face. "Got it."

"Just don't get sick in my car, all right?"

"It'd take a lot more than a mini-bottle to make me sick. Vodka's like water for me." She drained the bottle. "Been drinking it since I was thirteen."

He opened the Cheez-Its and ate some. "I want to hear more about this rebel-teenager Lola."

"She's still around, so don't provoke her," she said.

"I know you meant that as a threat, but I'm only more intrigued."

She turned her head toward the windshield. Everywhere she looked, there was something to see—a distant view of Los Angeles, the Big Dipper, the small one, the sandpaper mountains behind her. Beau.

"Maybe intrigued was too casual of a word," Beau teased. "Don't make me beg for more."

"I'm the same person I was then, just older. And maybe a little wiser."

"I may be older, but I don't feel any wiser," Beau said.

"Me neither," she said. "That was a lie." At the time, no matter how lost she'd been, she'd always thought she'd had it figured out. "What about you? Were you rebellious?"

"Nah. I was consumed by other things, like work, family and survival. Growing up poor really lights a fire under your ass. At least it did for me."

"I think everyone handles it differently. Your way of dealing was to take on all the responsibility. My mom was like that too, saddling the load on her back. Being poor was tough, but it made me stronger. I didn't let it rule my life."

"I bet you, Lola, were already strong to begin with."

"I was by myself a lot." She glanced over at him. Maybe it was the vodka, though she doubted it, but she was okay going places with him she hadn't been in a while. It was their space, like he'd said. "My mom wouldn't even take my birthdays off. Her reasoning was I'd only get a present if she had a job and she wouldn't have a job if she gave away shifts. When I said presents didn't matter, she asked me how I felt about food. For weeks I ate one meal a day because I was worried we'd run out."

Beau looked at the steering wheel. His hands balled and flexed against his thighs. "I wish you hadn't told me that. Things weren't that bad for us."

"They weren't for us either." They truly hadn't been, but she also had the urge to comfort him. "Looking back, it was never as dire as she made it seem. She hustled for her tips, and she never spent a dime on anything frivolous. The manager worshipped her, so she was never in jeopardy of losing her job. Our situation and our relationship fluctuated, but the one thing that stayed the same was that *she* thought there was never enough money. I couldn't do anything because there was no money. My father left because we—meaning I—cost him too much money."

"Is that true?" Beau asked.

"It's what she told me."

"He didn't explain to you why he left?"

"He went on a work trip and never came back. I don't think he was planning it because he left a lot of his stuff. I was too young to remember much anyway."

"Haven't seen him since?"

"No. So, like I said, alone a lot. Except at school. I didn't participate in a lot of stuff, but I had friends whether I wanted them or not. Then when I got home, it was silent. Nobody around. Except for Barbie fucker across the street."

"I'm not sure I like you hanging around with that girl."

Lola shook her head, smiling. "She was all right. Sometimes I wished I'd had a brother or sister, though. At least you had that."

"You wouldn't say that if you'd had Brigitte."

"Why not?"

"She was only fifteen when she moved here and had just lost her only family. She was so insecure about not belonging to anyone. She called me her brother from day one, and my mom 'Mom.' Unless she was angry, and then it was Pam. Looking back, it was something of a self-fulfilling prophecy. She didn't believe she deserved our love on top of our hospitality, and my mom already thought she was doing Brigitte this enormous favor by taking her in when we didn't have much to spare."

"No wonder she's a handful," Lola said.

He rested his head against the seat and looked up. "She was even before the accident. I didn't have to know her long to get that. Everything is extreme for Brigitte. Life. Love. Hate. She doesn't know who she is without that, and she thrives on the attention it gets her."

Lola frowned. "You're very close, aren't you?"

"She only has me. That's all she wants, though. Sometimes I give her projects at the office, and she usually does fine. I could never hire her fulltime, though—she's too volatile. I'm afraid others won't either. That's part of why I continue to help her. It's not a financial burden for me to take care of her when she has no one else. And after what my mom did, she has trust issues on top of that."

Lola peered at him in the dark. It was becoming clear that Beau had one sure way of showing he cared—his money. Earlier he'd said he'd given up years of his life to work, hoping one day he could provide for his family. The price didn't seem worth it, but she didn't think he felt the same.

"Your relationship doesn't sound healthy," Lola said. "For either of you."

"It's exhausting sometimes. She knows it is."

"Is she why you took me to a hotel rather than your house?"

He was silent a moment. "I've tried to get her a place of her own, but she cries and begs me not to. She says she'd rather one of us leave the house when she gets to be too much. As long as I don't go far. She gets more put out than I do, so I go through periods where I stay at the hotel."

Lola was instantly alarmed. If she hadn't known better, she would've thought Beau was describing a possessive girlfriend. "*That's* why you have the room? Jesus."

"I know. She just has two levels—low or high."

"Tonight was high?"

"Yes. She sniffed you out like a dog. Put her in a crowd, especially where men are involved, and she shines. One-on-one is more difficult. In case it's not obvious, she gets jealous of my attention."

Lola looked up at the stars. "I can understand that."

"Can you? You don't seem like the jealous type."

When Beau's attention was on her, Lola wasn't just the only girl in the room—she was the only girl in the world. It was intense—unnerving—but in an addictive way. She was warm when his eyes were on her, cold when they weren't. She shuddered.

He glanced at her. "Would you be jealous of my attention?"

Beau could most likely make any girl feel that way if he wanted. She squinted at nothing. "That would require thinking past tonight, and I don't want to."

"I'll be out there with other women, Lola. You'll be with Johnny. Everything will be normal again."

Things would never be normal again. Even if Johnny thought they were, or if she faked it until things were as close to normal as they'd get—no, they'd never truly be normal again. The question was whether Lola could live with that. "I don't know," she said. "All this has given me a lot to think about."

"Will I be there in those thoughts?"

He already was. She blinked a few times. "How could you not be? You started all of this."

"So what're you saying, Lola? You're going to go home and still be thinking about me?"

"Johnny and I…we're supposed to get through this on our love alone. On nine years' history. I think I knew we might not, but I called you anyway. When your limo pulled up tonight, it was as if Johnny and I had made some fatal mistake." She paused. "But I still went through with it."

Beau cleared his throat.

Lola noticed a symphony of crickets she hadn't before. She looked at him. "I mean, don't get the wrong idea," she said, flustered by his silence. This from the man who'd been so vocal, she'd wondered if he was considering going to battle with Johnny over her. "I'm not suggesting I leave him for you. It's just, the fact that Johnny and I even went through with this means something. Somebody owes somebody an explanation, I just don't know which one of us is at fault."

"I don't think it's anyone's fault," Beau said. "Not even mine."

She shook her head. "It isn't your fault." She couldn't pinpoint when she'd changed over the years, but she had. She'd thought putting her sordid past behind her meant she'd matured. Now she was beginning to question what part of the life she had now she'd chosen. Johnny had become her priority, and his hobbies, friends and work had become her hobbies, friends and work. She wanted more from herself and *for* herself, except that Johnny, with the greatest opportunity of his life ahead of him, still wasn't stepping up to the plate. "If things were right between Johnny and me, I wouldn't be here right now."

"I thought you were happy with him," Beau said. "At least it seemed that way from afar."

"I was," she said. "God, I *am*—I thought so. I had no idea anything was wrong. But you shook us up like a snow globe."

"If you're expecting an apology—"

"I'm not." She glanced at him and away.

"Lola," he called her attention back. "Come here."

She leaned across the console. He put an arm around her, pulling her close so their mouths nearly touched.

"Was I a fatal mistake?" he whispered.

"No." She shook her head slowly, holding his gaze. "Maybe."

He chuckled quietly.

"But don't think I'm going all psycho and dumping my boyfriend because of a couple nights of good sex."

Beau jerked his head back. "*Good?* Fuck. That hurts."

She rolled her eyes but smiled. "You know what I mean. Amazing."

"You can do better than that."

"You'll hold it against me."

"Probably."

Her smile widened. "Fine. Sex so good I think I went blind for a few seconds. Unparalleled sex."

"Unparalleled," he mused. "Meaning unmatched. Nobody can match it. Meaning…the best sex you've ever had."

She wriggled in his arms. "Don't get cocky on me."

"Hmm. I'd like to get cocky all over you," he muttered, brushing hair from her forehead. "Should we go back? Have you had your fill of stars?"

"Never," she said. "But it's not like we have eternity."

She went to pull away, but Beau's arm tightened as he kept her there.

"What?" she asked.

"I just wanted to say…I don't know what'll happen when the sun comes up—"

"I go home," she said, "is what happens."

He searched her face. "You should know how real this is for me." He took her cheek with his other hand. "If ever there were a prize worth winning, you are it. Just know that these stars, this moment—it's real. Everything I'm experiencing is real."

She looked back and forth between his eyes, trying to read him. There was truth there, but it wasn't the only thing. Something else brewed deeper. Something she didn't recognize. What did he want to tell her? To leave Johnny for him? He couldn't ask her to do it, but it was written on his face, woven in his touch.

"You don't have to say anything," Beau said. "We both knew what we were getting into. I just hope we each find what we need come sunrise."

What we need. Foolishly, she rarely considered what Beau needed, because he was always a pillar of strength. Maybe that was how Johnny saw her. Someone strong who didn't need much, and who was better at taking care of herself than anyone else would ever be.

She pushed Beau gently back against the driver's seat, keeping her eyes on his face. She felt under his T-shirt and up his flat stomach. He was warm and hard under her hand. His head fell back, and his eyes closed. His Adam's apple bobbed when he swallowed. "When's the last time someone touched you like this?"

He didn't answer.

"Not to get anything," she said. "Just to feel."

"A while," he said. The gravel in his voice made his answer almost unintelligible. "Maybe never."

She caressed his chest. To hear him say never made her heart sink, made her feel lucky for the years of tenderness Johnny had given her. "Let's go back to the hotel, Beau."

He blinked his eyes open, looking up for a minute. "We have a few hours. Maybe we can get some sleep."

"That'd be nice," she said.

He started the car.

She didn't tell him that she had no plans to sleep. That all she wanted to do was lie in his arms and try to stay awake.

Chapter Twelve

The drive back to Beau's hotel went quickly with the absence of traffic. On their way to Mulholland, there had been promise in the wind—now, just finality.

They took the exit for the hotel, and Beau pulled into a gas station and up to a pump. "I didn't feed you tonight," he said through her window once the tank was filling. "I'd planned on room service again."

Lola shrugged. "We had the Cheez-Its."

"Which is not all that bad of a dinner, but hardly fit for a queen." He winked. "Since I doubt there's French toast inside, how would you feel about gas station hotdogs?"

"Best with relish," she said.

"Then relish you will get. I'll be back in a minute."

Lola watched him walk away, enjoying every second of his firm behind in blue jeans. She caught herself grinning—over hotdogs. It lit her up from the inside that eating hotdogs was such a normal thing to do, as if they had all the time in the world. She didn't even particularly care for hotdogs, especially not ones that'd most likely been sitting on a rotisserie for the better part of a day. It was that she'd be having them with Beau.

But then she did start to think about the hotdogs themselves and how she actually was hungry, having eaten very little all night. Whenever she and Johnny took a trip, they'd stop for gas and sweets on their way out of town, even if they didn't particularly need gas. Johnny would get M&Ms but her cravings came in waves. She never knew what she was in the mood for until she saw it all in front of her. That was why she'd be the one to go get the candy while Johnny filled up the tank.

Now she couldn't stop thinking about chocolate, and Beau would have no idea what to get her. She didn't even know herself. She unbuckled her seatbelt and climbed out of the car. He'd paid for so much so far— dessert would be her treat. Beau probably had an old favorite, like Johnny. Men were like that. They found something that worked and stuck with it.

She pulled open the gas station door, walked in and stopped cold. Beau stood frozen at the counter, and a large, bearded man held a gun to his head. Beau's hands were clenched at his sides. The gas station attendant transferred cash from the register into a garbage bag.

"I told you, there isn't a single thing in my car," Beau was saying, his head slightly tilted as the barrel pressed into his temple. His eyes flickered to Lola and back. Slowly, he signaled with his hand for her to leave.

"Everything's on me. I have plenty of cash. I just need to reach in my pocket and get it."

"Which pocket?"

"Back right," Beau said.

Every beat of Lola's heart was acute. Rabid. She ached. He wouldn't hold her as she lay awake tonight. There wouldn't be a heartbreaking decision to make in the morning. They had fought each other, themselves, those around them—why? For it to end this way? She would've run to him if she could move. Her mouth was open, but she hadn't even been breathing.

"There's nothing here," the man said.

"Must be the left pocket." Beau widened his eyes at her, nodded once and mouthed, "Go." She barely registered that he was trying to distract the man from turning around.

"You're fucking with me." He reared back to hit Beau with the gun.

"I have it," Lola cried out. She couldn't even remember what she was supposed to have, her mind spun so fast. He wanted something. She would give it to him. Anything to change the picture in front of her— Beau, her strong, solid Beau, with a gun to his head.

The man whirled to her. "On the ground," he said.

He waved the gun back and forth, and when it stopped on her, her scalp went cold. His matted gray beard matched his leaden eyes, matched the pistol aimed at her face. His oversized army-green jacket had holes.

"Down," Beau ordered through his teeth. He gestured again, this time for her to lie on the floor. His dark eyes bore into her, willing her to submit.

She had to be brave. If she lay down, Beau would remain the target. She couldn't have that. Her breath came short as she looked between them.

"Listen, bitch." He put the barrel to Beau's head again. "This will be you if you don't get the fuck down."

Beau thrust his hand into his front pocket. "She's lying. My wallet's in—"

The man cocked the gun and shoved it harder into Beau's skull. "I told you not to move, motherfucker. Put it in the bag and do it slow."

Beau slid it out and dropped it in with the rest of the money.

"Now you," he said, nodding at Lola. "Throw your purse over here."

As long as the gun was on Beau, she saw nothing else. All it would take was a slip of the finger, a burst of anger. "Not until you put the gun down."

"Who the fuck you think's in charge?" the man asked.

She held up her purse, waving it as if he were a bear and she had his dinner. The man was off—he could snap at any moment, but if he did, she'd make sure that gun was pointed anywhere but at Beau. Even if it was aimed at her instead. "If you want it, come take it from me."

"Throw the fucking purse," Beau said sharply.

Purse. Wallet. Money. Her brain began to thaw. "I have cash." Her legs wobbled. She took a step back and raised her chin. "I just came from the ATM."

He looked from Beau to Lola and back before walking toward her.

Beau lunged, but the man was fast. He spun around and trained the weapon on Beau again. He backed his way to Lola, feeling for her with the same hand he clutched the garbage bag in. She couldn't tell how lucid he was. She didn't want to test him, so she stayed where she was. He grabbed her shirt and pulled her in front of him, wrapping an arm around her shoulders and jamming the cold muzzle under her chin, forcing her head up. He slid his hand down her stomach. "Give it to me."

The barrel pressed into her throat when she swallowed. She tried not to cough and instead inhaled a wilting blend of urine, body odor and hard alcohol. Without moving more than she had to or looking down, she surrendered the purse.

"She and I are going to walk out," he said to Beau. "If you want to keep her alive, don't make any moves until I'm gone. Got it?"

"I lied," Beau said hastily. He was below her line of vision, on her peripheral, but there was clear desperation in his voice. "About the car. And what's in it. I can get you anything you want. I have more money than you can dream of."

The man released the gun just enough for Lola's head to drop. Beau flexed his hands in and out of balls, imploring her with his eyes. She couldn't read him, and that made her stomach churn. She had no idea what he might do.

"How much we talking here?" the man smacked in her ear.

"Millions. All yours if you just let her go. I'll go out to the car with you instead."

Lola held her breath, sucking in her nostrils to prevent smelling anything.

He laughed. "Now I *know* you're fucking with me." He pulled Lola backward with him.

Beau, as if connected by a string, walked forward also. "Look outside," Beau pressed. "That's my Lamborghini. You can have it too. Outrun the cops, no problem."

Lola didn't dare check to see if the man looked.

The man whistled in Lola's ear. "You weren't kidding. Keys in the car?"

Beau patted his pockets. "Yes."

"You stay here while we check," he said, dragging Lola backward with him. "Everything's good, I'll let her go."

"Leave her," Beau said levelly.

"Nope. She's my collateral."

"The car is nothing." Beau's jaw clenched and unclenched, causing his face to contort. The gun was still on her, between her and Beau, putting them on opposites sides of danger. "I can get you so much more. We don't have to get the cops involved. Just let go of her."

Lola couldn't hold her breath anymore, and she gagged.

"What's wrong, little lady?" the man asked tauntingly. "You know, there's one thing you've got that he can't give me." He squeezed her more tightly against him.

She'd die before she let that happen. Before she could gag again, she grabbed his forearm. "Let go of me."

"Shut up," he said with a hard shake.

Beau's hands had stopped moving. His expression smoothed as any emotion drained away, leaving his eyes colder than she'd ever seen them. His back became unnaturally straight. "You might want to rethink who you're pointing that gun at," he said. "I don't think you realize how much you've just pissed me off."

A wave of panic crashed through Lola. He had the same indifferent look he'd had the night Johnny had gone after him at Hey Joe. It was the complete inability to predict his next move that terrified her—not that he'd do anything to jeopardize her, but that he wasn't thinking of his own safety at all.

Beau strode forward, each step longer than the last. The man pushed the gun into Lola's throat then pulled it away. It wavered in the air a split second as he seemed to hesitate. He pointed it at Beau and shot. Lola screamed. Shoved back into a display stand, she lost her footing and fell as it crashed around her. Beau was at her side in an instant, yelling at her, but all she heard was the reverberation of the gunshot.

Frantically, she reached up and felt his chest. "He shot you?"

He grabbed her arm, checked her over and left her on the ground. He ran back to the counter and lunged over it, reaching for the attendant.

"Beau," she said lamely, unsure he could even hear her. "What are you doing?"

Beau grabbed the kid by his shirt and pulled him forward. He was tearing something from the guy's hand—a gun. He was going after the man. Dread rose up her throat.

He bolted for the door. She scrambled to her feet, hurtling into his path. "It's just money. It's not worth it," she cried.

He went to move around her, but she grabbed his shirt in two tight fists. Now that she had him back, she couldn't risk losing him again. "Please, I'm begging you. Don't do this."

"It's not about the money," he said, his face bright red, his chest heaving. "I won't let him get away with this."

"I need you here," she said. "Don't abandon me."

He glanced anxiously behind her. "I can't just do nothing. I'll come right back."

She couldn't shake the thought that he'd been shot. Her chin wobbled. "You might not come back." Her strength seeped away, leaving her knees weak. His arms automatically went around her waist, and the gun pressed through the back of her T-shirt, cold even through the fabric. "Let the police handle it. Stay."

"He deserves to pay," Beau said through clenched teeth. "You're asking me to let it go? People don't just get away with this. He could've killed you, Lola. He deserves to run for his life—from *me*."

He was like a wolf separated from fresh meat with only Lola in between. His heartbeat was strong under his chest, and all his muscles were tensed as if he might break into a sprint at any instant.

He wanted payback. Why couldn't he see the gift they'd been given? A second chance? He would risk his life to make an insane man pay—for what? They were both unharmed. She shook him by his shirt. "*I* don't deserve to lose *you*. Not after all this. I need you here where I can see you and touch you. If you go, I go with you."

He opened his mouth, trying to speak but nothing came out at first.

"If you go, I go," she repeated.

"But he...and you..." His face closed. "What the hell were you thinking?" he demanded. "Why didn't you leave when you had the chance? Why didn't you just do what he said?"

She would take all of Beau's anger if it meant keeping him there in that building. Her fingers loosened with her relief. "Why didn't you let him take me outside?"

He looked up at the ceiling. "You know why."

"Then you know why I couldn't leave you here."

There was a word for that, but Lola couldn't let it form in her mind. If she did, she'd never see clearly again. They stared at each other, both breathing deeply.

He detangled from her finally and went to turn away, but reached back and took her arm. "Do not leave my side." He walked them up to the counter where he placed the gun down but didn't release it. He kept his other hand on Lola. The attendant was on the phone with the police.

"Tell them we can still catch the guy," Beau said, glancing at the door. "And to hurry the fuck up."

"Beau?" Lola asked.

"Not now. I have to do this." He let her go and took the phone right out of the kid's hand. "Is someone on the way?" he asked and waited. "Every second that passes, he gets farther away. I don't even know—"

Sirens sounded out front.

"Never mind," Beau said, dropping the receiver.

He took two steps before the attendant called after him. "Dude, my gun. You go out there with that and they'll turn you into Swiss cheese."

Beau rubbed his forehead tensely and looked at his hand.

"Put it down," Lola said. "He's not coming back."

He slid it across the counter to the attendant. "Stay here," he said to Lola. He didn't move a moment, then took her shoulders firmly. "Do you hear me, Lola? Don't try and be brave. Just stay put until I come get you."

He was afraid. Now that her sense had returned, she was too. She nodded quickly, breathlessly. "I won't move."

His fingers loosened, but he wouldn't stop looking at her. "You really fucking scared me, you know that? This is why I never stray from the plan—not ever."

She searched his face. "What plan?"

"There's always a plan, Lola. Tonight was about you and me, and that's why I wanted to stay in the hotel room. Just be with you. This is all my fault for not sticking to the plan."

"But it was my idea," she said.

He pulled her against him hard and hugged her. He buried his face in her hair. "Goddamn it," he whispered.

He released her all at once and strode out of the convenience store. The attendant was already in front. She stood frozen to the spot. Her breathing hadn't calmed. Her heart felt like it was bottoming out.

She'd almost lost everything in minutes. Her life. Her future. Their future. Beau. She shook her head. He wasn't everything. He was just a man she'd spent two nights with. A man she'd already been planning to say goodbye to in a few hours.

She'd risked her life for that man. For a man she'd never see again after tonight. And he—he had done the same by not letting her out of his sight, even to save himself.

She'd almost lost him in minutes. He was everything.

There was a word for that—it was *love*.

◆ ◆ ◆

The car dipped as they entered the hotel's underground garage. The gun's cold metal was still under Lola's chin. She wanted Beau's touch to replace it. To replace the last hour of being separated from him as policemen questioned each of them. Lola rubbed her hands up and down her thighs. She'd stopped shaking, but she was jittery.

Beau pulled into a parking spot and shut off the car. "In the morning, we'll—" He stopped.

What, go get a bite to eat? Give the credit card companies a call? Pick her up a replacement cell phone? That wasn't their life. Their life followed the sun's schedule, and it would be waking up soon. "In the morning, we'll nothing," she said. "Nothing."

They were silent. The police had asked if Beau was her boyfriend. Where they'd been. Where they were going. Why they needed a hotel if they lived in Los Angeles. The dashboard in front of Lola blurred and doubled. She breathed in and out.

What would they have said if she'd told them the truth?

"We're not what you think, Officer. He's paying me to be here right now. In this gas station. I'm being paid for this."

She didn't want Beau's money. She could give it back and not leave in the morning, but then there was Johnny. Johnny, who hadn't protected her. He hadn't known if Beau would hurt her, or if she'd come home in one piece. He'd sent her off into a potentially dangerous situation—twice. *He* would've let the man with the gun take her outside to save his ass.

She undid her seatbelt.

"Lola?" Beau asked.

She put a knee over the console and climbed onto him. He didn't protest, just took her hips as she settled into his lap. She put her hands on both sides of his face and kissed him. He was solid. Real. Immovable. He tasted salty. One of them was crying.

"It's okay to be scared," Beau whispered. "You don't have to be strong all hours of the day."

"For you." She was trembling again, but this time it wasn't because of the gun. She couldn't say goodbye to him. She wouldn't. She'd walked into the gas station. He'd had a gun to his head. It was branded into her heart. His stubble scraped against her fingertips and her palms. She might've never felt that again.

"I was scared for you," she said, her tears sliding down both their cheeks. "Scared something would happen to you."

His arms tightened around her. "We're both safe now," he said in a humming, soothing voice. "I'll keep you safe."

He had needs too. She kissed his lips, his cheek. "What about you? Who will keep you safe?"

"You did, Lola."

She shuddered. If she had saved him, it was to protect herself. She couldn't live without knowing if all of her life had been leading up to this moment. She stayed in his lap, dug her fingers into his face and released. She fought herself.

"What is it?" he asked, his eyebrows heavy. "We're running out of time."

She reached for his fly to undo it, but stopped. Sobs racked her body. She fisted his shirt, stretching it. There was everything, and there was everything else. Beau had remained solid through it all. Beau had been strong and unwavering. Beau was hers. Nobody was going to take him away from her.

She clung to him. "I'm falling in love with you."

He stilled completely. It was dark, but his eyes were green as they looked up into hers. She felt his chest again, as if checking for a bullet wound. He slid his hands down her back and into the seat of her pants, pulling her against him. Their lips met fast and hot like flames licking at their faces, every touch gasoline on the fire. He opened her jeans, yanking them down over and over, trying to get to her. She had to lift her knee to get one pant leg off so he could angle upward, his own pants barely undone, to find his way inside her. He took control of her hips, pushing her down on him. There wasn't even time to moan, to think, to do anything but feel him hard and filling her.

"Look at me and say it," Beau said.

She found his eyes with hers. They weren't words, just breaths. "I love you."

He pulled on the neckline of her T-shirt, grabbed her breasts. She arched into his hands, throwing her back against the steering wheel. The horn honked and her jeans ripped somewhere and she was coming as hard as he was thrusting up into her. He groaned louder and louder until he also came.

She reached out to grab onto anything. Her palm connected with the cold window, her other hand landing on his heaving chest. They were real things, unlike love, unlike fear, which she couldn't hold.

The car was closing in on her. She opened the door and would've tumbled out if Beau hadn't caught her waist. She slapped his hands away and stood. It took her three fumbling tries to get back into her jeans. She ran both hands through her hair. "Fuck," she screamed. It bounced off the gray, concrete walls. Nothing had ever seemed as dire. She loved two men, but she loved them differently. With Johnny, it was in a way that she'd let him go before she returned with only part of the heart that had belonged to him. With Beau, her love wasn't that selfless. It was an annihilation of her senses. A conquest, a theft of her entire self. She squatted between two painted white lines and pulled hard on her hair. "I'm so fucked," she said between hitched breaths, rocking back and forth.

A car door slammed, echoing around the garage. Beau walked up next to her.

This had to be her moment alone. She deserved to do this on her own for the way she'd led everyone into this mess. She could've ended it all with a firm, simple *no*. "Go away. I can't do this right now."

"I'm not going anywhere."

"I mean it," she said.

"You're in the middle of a parking spot." He leaned down to help her up, but she jumped to her feet. He had tricked her. Pulled the wool over her eyes. It was the only explanation. She hadn't even tried to keep love out of it, because love hadn't been an option. It had blindsided her completely. She shoved him backward. "I said go. I hate you."

He took two large steps and grabbed her wrists before she could push him again.

"I hate you for this," she said. "You ruined everything. We were fine before you. We were happy."

"You said it yourself—you wouldn't be here if that were true." He forced her against his chest where she broke down and bawled. He wrapped his arms around her, rubbing her back with his large hand.

"Nobody has ever made me feel so alone," she said.

He pulled away slightly. "I make you feel *alone*?"

She'd learned her lesson as a kid when her dad had walked out on her and her mom—the only person she could rely on was herself. Not even Johnny or her mom. But she couldn't see beyond tomorrow, beyond Beau, when she'd have to go back to a life that had been fine before him. "I could always take care of myself. I've never needed anyone." She wouldn't look at him. "I haven't even left yet, and I already feel alone."

Even she didn't trust herself. Just yesterday, it'd been Johnny she'd loved. Nothing could erase that, but their love had stopped growing somewhere along the way—not because it hadn't been nourished or tended to, but because from the start, it could only get so big.

What she felt for Beau was new, but already it seemed as though it could reach a terrifying size. It couldn't be trimmed, monitored or kept. It was a vine that had the potential to overtake everything in its path. Lola didn't know which of the two was the right kind, only that after glimpsing the possibility of her and Beau, a stunted love with Johnny wouldn't be enough anymore.

Beau covered her hair with both hands. His grip was firm, but his words were soft. "I don't want you to feel alone."

She looked up finally. "What do you want me to feel?"

"Loved."

"Johnny loves me."

His eyes darted between hers. The garage was silent except for the one rapid heartbeat between them. He opened his mouth and shut it. He put a hand on her cheek. "Lola."

He said her name so thickly, she could almost reach out and touch it. Her fingertips tingled. She was back in the drugstore as a teenager about to commit a crime. She wouldn't stand in the way anymore. She wanted him. She'd chained it up inside early on, but it was coming loose. If Johnny had fought for her at all, Beau had fought harder.

His eyebrows gathered as he frowned down at her. "Sometimes I think you can see through things other people can't. You see me. You make me powerful, but more," he paused, swallowing, as if the words were fighting within him, "you make me powerless."

Powerless. That was what she'd seen in his eyes when she couldn't read him. It wasn't that he'd been asking anything of her, but that he'd been unable to do anything for her, and Beau thrived on his power.

"And I don't want to put you in that car at sunrise," he said.

"You don't?"

"No, but I have to. It's our agreement."

"I don't care about the money," she said. "I love you. I love him. Tell me what to do, Beau. I'll do it."

"Okay." He was dependable. He made decisions in her best interest, not his. Even when he commanded her, he did it to give her things she hadn't known she wanted. He smoothed his hand lovingly over her hair until he was cupping the back of her head. "Here's what you're going to do, Lola. You're going to go home. You're going to tell Johnny it's over."

Involuntarily, she curled her hands harder into his T-shirt. They were two distinct concepts in her mind. There was loving Beau, and there was ending it with Johnny. They'd been two mutually exclusive ideas, one she was submitting to and one she hadn't seriously entertained. Beau wanted to merge them. "Just like that? Over?"

"Isn't it?" he asked. "How can you be with him after this?"

She shook her head. "How can I do that to him?"

"I told you once, you can't sacrifice yourself to make him happy. You know what you want, but somewhere along the way, he helped you bury your instinct. Go there again. What does it tell you?"

Her heart swelled. Johnny liked Lola's edge, but it was true. He preferred her a little dulled. Beau, on the other hand, wanted what he'd been asking for all along—her. He hadn't even put one day between meeting her and making his proposition. Within an hour of their sidewalk encounter, he'd told her she had his attention. His assurance was in his actions. Maybe he'd known all along. Maybe this had always been his plan. It was the reason she'd been pressing him for. He'd chosen her because he was a man who knew what he wanted.

"My instinct tells me that Johnny and I have history," she said, "but that he's not my future."

"And why not?" he prompted.

"Because you are."

Chapter Thirteen

Back on the sixteenth floor, Lola and Beau went about their tasks. It was time to return her to Johnny. Her rightful owner. She showered again to rid herself completely of the man with the gun and gathered her things while Beau changed. When she was ready, she sat on the edge of the bed.

Beau hung up his phone and set it on the nightstand next to her. "Warner'll be here in a few minutes," he said, looking down at her. "I'm not coming with you."

He was having seconds thoughts. No—she had to trust him. She took a deep breath. "How come?"

"I want you back here tonight." He rubbed his forehead with tense fingers. "Warner will sit out front until you're ready while I take care of things here. I have the suite as long as we need it. Leave whatever you don't need there. We can figure the rest out once this is done."

"I don't think I can just walk in there, get my things and walk back out," she said.

"That's why I can't go. Warner will wait as long as it takes, though. I don't want you staying overnight there, Lola."

He was shifting back into business mode as the night dissolved into dawn. Lola bit her bottom lip. "Are you sure about this?"

He didn't answer right away. He reached out, fingered a piece of her hair and tucked it behind her ear. With his thumb and forefinger, he lifted her chin. "I'm not Johnny. I don't waver in my decisions. I don't backtrack. I don't put anything on your shoulders if I can help it. If I could do this part for you, I would. Yes, I'm sure."

She drew on his strength, lengthening her spine and holding his gaze. "I can do this part myself. It won't be easy, but I can do it if you're waiting for me."

He smiled. "There's the girl on the sidewalk I had to have. The one who kicks cars and doesn't apologize."

She nodded, but hard as she fought it, her mind was creeping ahead of the moment. It was in her apartment, waking Johnny up from a dream to plunge him into a nightmare. "I think it's best I call Johnny to let him know I'm on my way."

"Why?"

"He should be completely awake for this conversation. I'll tell him to have coffee ready."

Beau raised his eyebrows at her. "You're telling me he's asleep right now? While you're here with me, he's *asleep*?"

If things went like they had her first night with Beau, Johnny would be sleeping off his drunkenness. She shook her head. "It's a good thing. He'd drive himself crazy otherwise."

Beau sighed and pointed at the nightstand. "Your cell phone was in your purse?"

"Yes."

"Use mine. Also—" He paused, hedging. "The other half of your money's in the closet. I was also going to give it to you in cash."

"Was?" she asked.

"Like I said, I've never broken the terms of an agreement, but I'm making an exception on this point. Understand me when I say—I don't have many regrets in my life, but making you feel worthless is one of them. This money does not belong to you because you did not earn it. You are not this money. Understand me?"

It was all she'd wanted to hear since this thing had started, she just hadn't realized it until then. That she, her love, was worth more than any dollar amount. Lola's chest ached. "I don't want it."

"Good." He put his hands on his hips and dropped his forehead toward the floor. After a deep breath, he opened his mouth. "There's something else—" He shook his head. Paused. Cleared his throat.

"What else?"

"Nothing. Never mind. We can talk later."

It was a rare thing to see him nervous. It could've been because of what they were about to do, but it almost seemed like something else. "Talk about what?" she asked warily.

"Everything. There's a lot to figure out, but now you'd better go." He walked away. "I'll grab shoes and walk you down."

She had to make the call. Lola's body was a tornado of emotion. Her heart beat so hard, it practically reached for Beau as he disappeared into the closet. Her stomach, on the other hand, was in knots. It was not a conversation she'd ever pictured herself having with Johnny, but now she couldn't imagine not doing it. She'd made the decision to leave him so quickly that she wondered if it'd been waiting just below the surface, and if so, for how long.

She picked up Beau's phone. As she dialed Johnny's cell phone, a text message from Brigitte popped up.

Good luck this morning. Remember what I said last night. Stick to the plan. The bitch is just getting what she deserves. Can't wait to hear all about it tonight. See you downstairs. xo

Lola read it one more time before the screen went black. *Bitch? Deserves?* Her throat closed. Her hand had begun to shake. It was possible the text wasn't about her at all, yet it was even more possible that it was—unless Beau was giving someone else what they deserved this morning, and Lola doubted that would be much better. Just moments ago she'd told herself to trust Beau, but that was already crumbling. She stood up in one jerky movement.

Beau emerged from the closet. "Ready?" he asked, patting his pockets. "Oh, I left my phone—" He glanced up at Lola, who'd raised the phone in front of her with the screen toward him.

"What is this?" she asked.

Beau's expression cleared as if he knew instantly. "Lola." He held out his hands, either to placate or reach for her. "What did you see? What does it say?"

"A text message from Brigitte."

He looked up at the ceiling, swallowed and exhaled. "No. You have got to be fucking kidding me."

She couldn't breathe. Any doubt she'd had that the text wasn't about her was gone. Lola gripped the phone until her knuckles were white. "What do I deserve? What plan?"

He looked at her again. "Listen to me. If I tell you the truth like this, you won't understand." He put his hands palm to palm in front of him. "Trust me on this. Go home. Talk to Johnny. When you come back, I'll explain everything."

That was the reverse of how she wanted to do things. She had everything on the line as she was about to throw nine years down the drain. "Do you honestly think I'm that stupid? Don't tell me you'll explain this *after* I uproot my life for you."

"You don't want to hear the truth," Beau said with warning. "You have to trust me here, Lola."

"I can't."

"You *can't?*" he asked. "You put yourself in front of that gun for me tonight, and now you can't trust me?"

Her eyes darted over the floor. She'd done it without hesitation, and he'd protected her too. At least, she'd thought he had.

But there was a plan.

And it involved her.

"There's always a plan, Lola."

The text message was casual, as if it were nothing for Brigitte to call Lola a bitch to Beau—the man who was asking her to trust him. Her decision maker. The man who'd demanded her surrender and who'd received it. She was in his hands, and she trusted him, but in that text, Brigitte had a reason to believe Beau wasn't on Lola's side.

"No," she said. "Before I walk into my home with the intention to walk right back out, I need you to tell me exactly what Brigitte meant by that."

He took a threatening step toward her. "You aren't the only one uprooting your life. You think this has been easy for me? Letting someone in who's in love with another man?"

"You shouldn't have," she said, her voice rising. "I didn't ask you for that. I didn't want any of this."

"And *I* wasn't the one who was supposed to—" He stopped.

"Supposed to what?" she asked after a silence, but he only stared at her. "Come on, Beau. Tell me what the plan was. Tell me what I was supposed to do that I didn't." She grit her teeth. "I did *everything* you asked. I fought you tooth and nail but I gave you what you wanted."

"Yes," he said. "You did everything right."

"So what is it then?" She cocked her head. The longer he clung to the truth, the more Lola had to know. Whatever it was, he wasn't going to give it up easily, which meant she needed to go deeper. "Maybe it's not what I *didn't* do, but what I did."

His jaw set. "What do you mean?"

"Power is a funny thing, isn't it? Sometimes the one who thinks he holds it…doesn't hold it at all."

He shook his head in warning, narrowing his darkened eyes on her. "Don't."

"That's it, isn't it? You want to love me more than you want to control me, and it scares you. You'd let me have that power to keep me."

"Nobody has that over me," he clipped.

"Someone did tonight," she said, raising an eyebrow. "That man could've taken everything from you with one bullet."

He stepped closer to her. "He didn't, because we protected each other. We were in control. I'm still in control."

"That's fine, Beau. Control isn't what I want. I want truth. You can keep your ridiculous obsession with having it all."

"Ridiculous?" he asked, his nostrils flaring. "You think power comes over night? You think I decide? No. I fucking earned it. I've worked my ass off so people would respect me. So I could buy you expensive dresses and drive you around in a car people would literally kill to have. That man tonight—he could've killed you if he'd taken you out there, all for what I have."

"Who says I want any of that?" she countered, pushing back against his anger. "I could give a crap about your car or your empty lifestyle. Without it, you're just you, and that scares you. I make you powerless."

"Are you fucking kidding me?" He charged forward, and she retreated until her legs hit the bed. He snatched the phone away, launching it against a wall as she flinched. His large shoulders moved up and down as he breathed hard. "I can't *believe* I let you get to me like this again."

"Again—?"

"You're so righteous, aren't you, Lola?" He towered over her. "You don't need or want anything like the rest of us. You can't be bought. Your pussy's not for sale."

She flushed. He made her sound high and mighty for that, as if any other woman would've rolled over and given him what he wanted. She had nowhere to put her hands, so she covered her stomach.

He laughed, and it was as hollow as his eyes. That emptiness was even more frightening than his indifference had been. "You were wrong. You said it couldn't be done, but *I* did it. Me."

"What did you do?" she asked, dread softening her voice. Suddenly she didn't want to challenge or push him—she just wanted him to be himself again.

"Imagine this, Lola. Ten years ago, it's the biggest moment of my life—what everything else has led up to. I've just signed a contract to sell one of the companies I practically killed myself to build. For years, I've denied myself everything for work—women, fun, sleep, life. It doesn't matter, though, because it's finally paid off. I'm going to be a multi-millionaire.

"I want to celebrate," he continued. "But I have no one. I'm alone. So I walk into a strip club looking for anybody, but I see this girl on stage with long, black hair and kitten ears on her head—furry black triangles. She looks over her shoulder and directly at me with the bluest eyes. She's got this body men *kill* for and is wearing a fucking—are you still with me?" He gestured up and down at her. "It looks like a bikini made of goddamn diamonds. It's so bright, it almost blinds me when the spotlight is on her. She's the most stunning thing I've ever seen. I have to have her. *Her.*" He pointed into the distance. "*That one.* I pay for Cat Shoppe's most expensive room. I pay to see her dance, for her attention. She gets so close to me that our legs touch, even though that isn't allowed. She's flirting. I tell her I need her—I'll do anything, *pay* anything for her. I offer her a grand, but she shakes her head. Five grand. She just smiles. Ten thousand dollars. She looks me right in my eyes, bats her lashes like a little cunt and says—"

"I'm not for sale," Lola whispered.

"That's right," he said. "But you were wrong, weren't you?"

Lola wavered on her legs, reaching back to steady herself on the mattress. She narrowed her eyes on him, recalling the young, handsome man from that night. "That was you at Cat Shoppe." Her entire body shook. "You knew who I was on the sidewalk at Hey Joe?"

"Yes."

"Why? Why are you doing this?"

"You thought you were too good for money I broke my back to earn. Because you couldn't give me that one fucking thing on the most important night of my life. Because—" He faltered, leveling his eyes on her.

For a brief second, he looked as pained as she felt. The whole thing was made even more shocking by the fact that there were depths to him she hadn't even scratched.

He'd earned that money so he would be enough. So nobody could turn him down or walk away from him, because in his eyes, everybody had a price. Perhaps he was right. She'd once thought she could never be bought, no matter the amount.

"I hurt you," she said, hating the break in her voice.

The pained look vanished. "I promised myself nobody would ever make me feel that way again. There would be nothing my money couldn't buy. And then there you were again out front of Hey Joe, just as beautiful as that night ten years ago. It was like no time had passed. And when you returned my tip and insisted there was no connection between us, I was just as weak." He splayed his hands over his chest. "You're the only person who does this to me, Lola. You're a threat to everything I've worked for."

She shook her head. "I'm not a threat. I didn't hurt you on purpose. You...you can't do this."

"It's done. I've proven anything can be bought. Today, I get back the power you took from me."

"I am not a thing to be overcome. I'm a person." She clutched her throat. Her skin was burning. "If this were true, you would've told me after the first night."

"I tried, believe me." He crossed his arms. "But you, so stubborn, had to go and say that buying someone's body didn't count. It had to be their heart." He hesitated only a moment, but he'd gone too far down whatever path he was on. He couldn't seem to stop himself, even as Lola's heart broke right in front of him. "I was going to end it there, but you wanted to play. And as you know, I'm not one to turn down a challenge. She thinks her heart isn't for sale? I'll buy that too, I thought. You only have yourself to blame for loving me."

A challenge. That's what this had been about. Conquering her, teaching her a lesson, winning a game. He'd been dropping hints along the way, most likely for his own amusement. "Fuck you," she uttered. "You think my life is a game?"

He uncrossed his arms and ran both hands along the bridge of his nose. "It was until it wasn't. I realized tonight, with you in my arms, telling me you love me, how wrong I've been. But I promise you, from the first minute, I meant everything I said, Lola. I never lied about how I felt. I want you—"

She scrambled back so fast when he reached for her that she landed on the bed. "Don't you dare fucking touch me."

He grabbed the comforter on both sides of her and pulled it, sliding her back toward him. He jerked her to her feet by her biceps. "You want to test me? You'll lose. Want to fucking run away from me? You can't. Fight me all you want." He kissed her hard. "Hurt me. I can take it. But you can't outrun me. You're strong, but you're not strong enough to take me on. You might as well give in."

Her knees threatened to buckle. There was undiluted pain and frustration in his voice. He loved her, even if he couldn't say it. She loved him. And she'd never wanted to hurt anyone worse in her life. She looked him in the eye and said, "I want my money."

It took a moment for anything to register on his face. His mouth parted. "Your *money*?"

She had to fight not to look away from him. He'd hurt her, and words were all she had. She struggled to push him off. "That's all you're good for. All I am is my pussy and all you are is your money. So give it to me so I can go."

He tightened his grip. "That's not true, and you know it. That isn't what we are."

She dug deeper. Sank her claws into her pain. What he'd done deserved her worst. "Go buy some more people, and get the fuck out of my life. Build your empire and run it all by yourself. Alone. No matter how much money you spend, you will never have me, and you and I will never have what Johnny and I do."

He tilted his head with a jerk as if his lid were about to fly off. "Liar. Earlier you said—"

"Earlier I was hysterical," she spat. "I thought I was going to die. I don't even know what I was saying. I love Johnny, and I just want to go home to him."

He raised his chin, looking down at her. His jaw worked back and forth as he breathed through his nose. He pushed her backward hard and stormed to the closet. Her chest stuttered viciously as if collapsing in on itself. She wanted to run away from him and to him in equal parts. She needed to believe in his arms around her, but every time he'd touched her, it was a lie. It was to get something from her—not just something, but the most valuable thing she had to give. Her heart.

He reappeared with a brown package like the one he'd brought to her apartment the night before. "Here's the other five hundred grand," he said, tossing it. It landed with a heavy thump at her feet. "Now get the fuck out."

She only needed to be strong long enough to leave that presidential suite in one piece. The money was heavier than she expected, and she had to heave it from the floor into her arms. She walked right up to him, standing under his nose. "Coward. There's a reason you had to have *me* that night and a reason you're still thinking about *me* ten years later, and it wasn't to win some stupid game."

"You're probably right. And it's the same reason you're still standing here when I told you to leave."

She gripped the package until her fingers hurt. "You could've had me without the money," she said. "You could've come back for me, but you were too scared to even try. Now you've lost me. I took your power, and that means you've lost your game."

He didn't shy away from her anger. His green eyes fixed on her, the thick of the forest, the dark, inconceivable pit. He was a monster, but a beautiful one with his sharp, dimpled chin and mussed coffee-bean hair. If only, with his confession, he'd also been forced to shed the mask he'd used to lure her in.

"You're wrong. I haven't lost anything," he said. "Because I'm not the one who fell in love."

"Yes, you did. I want to hear you say it. You made me say it, you fucking coward. Now you say it."

"You will never hear me say it," he said. "Get out."

He might as well have slapped her. She almost wished he had, because at least then she'd be able to feel her pain in a physical way, instead of as a gaping hole in her chest. "You can thank Brigitte for me. She saved me from making the biggest mistake of my life."

Lola left the room. She had somewhere to be and not long now to get there.

But she wasn't finished with Beau. He'd committed the greatest crime there was—he'd played with love. And nobody should ever be able to get away with that.

He'd made mistakes, thinking she hadn't been paying attention, but she had. He'd exposed his weakness to her and handed her the weapon she needed.

He survived on power—she would take it from him.

He was in love with her—she would use that to do it.

As she rode the elevator down to the ground floor, she made a decision. Somehow, some way, Beau would get what he deserved. She would break him too, and she'd do it without the mercy he'd tried to afford her.

He'd hidden behind his money so long, he'd never let anyone close enough to hurt him. Except for her. She was there. She was certain that he loved her—and that he'd come to regret it.

She wasn't sure how.

She wasn't sure when.

She only knew one thing.

Beau Olivier would be sorry he'd ever laid eyes on her.

BOOKS IN THE

Explicitly Yours Series

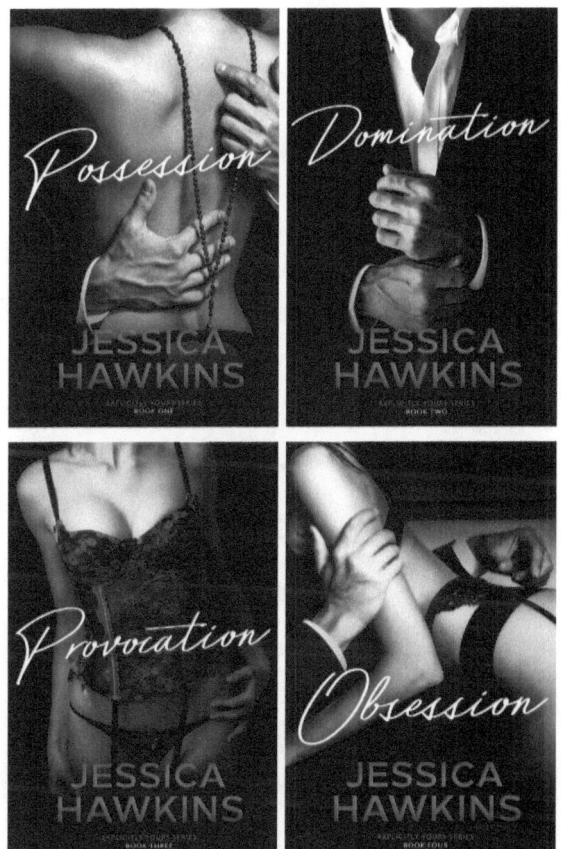

LEARN MORE AT
JESSICAHAWKINS.NET/EYSERIES

TITLES BY
JESSICA HAWKINS

LEARN MORE AT JESSICAHAWKINS.NET/BOOKS

SLIP OF THE TONGUE
THE FIRST TASTE
YOURS TO BARE

THE CITYSCAPE SERIES
COME UNDONE
COME ALIVE
COME TOGETHER

EXPLICITLY YOURS SERIES
POSSESSION
DOMINATION
PROVOCATION
OBSESSION

STRICTLY OFF LIMITS

ABOUT THE AUTHOR

JESSICA HAWKINS grew up between the purple mountains and under the endless sun of Palm Springs, California. She studied international business at Arizona State University and has also lived in Costa Rica and New York City. To her, the most intriguing fiction is forbidden, and that's what you'll find in her stories. Currently, she resides wherever her head lands, which is often the unexpected (but warm) keyboard of her trusty MacBook.

CONNECT WITH JESSICA

Stay updated & join the
JESSICA HAWKINS Mailing List
www.JESSICAHAWKINS.net/mailing-list

www.amazon.com/author/jessicahawkins
www.facebook.com/jessicahawkinsauthor
twitter: @jess_hawk

www.ingramcontent.com/pod-product-compliance
Lightning Source LLC
Chambersburg PA
CBHW032131170626
46808CB00006B/2181